PUBLISH OR DIE

"Just keep your head down, dear," Romy advised. "Publishing's not the genteel world that people imagine. Dale may give the impression of being a bit of a fop, but underneath that suave, ever-so-English exterior, he's a tough cookie. He and Elizabeth have had some real fights."

"From what I read in those memos," said Calico, "it looks like there's another one on the way – with Austen Porter."

"Elizabeth doesn't pull her punches," Romy remarked, ruefully. "When she takes offence to something, her bite is every bit as bad as her bark." She nodded and opened her eyes wide. "Austen better beware. They'd *all* better beware…"

Look out for:

Patsy Kelly Investigates: Death By Drowning
Anne Cassidy

The Beat: Night Shift
David Belbin

Lawless & Tilley: Still Life
Malcolm Rose

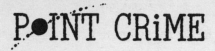

POINT CRIME

PUBLISH OR DIE

Alan Durant

■SCHOLASTIC

Scholastic Children's Books
Commonwealth House, 1–19 New Oxford Street,
London WC1A 1NU, UK
a division of Scholastic Ltd
London ~ New York ~ Toronto ~ Sydney ~ Auckland

First published in the UK by Scholastic Ltd, 1998

Copyright © Alan Durant, 1998

ISBN 0 590 19395 3

Typeset by TW Typesetting, Midsomer Norton, Somerset
Printed by Cox & Wyman Ltd, Reading, Berks.

10 9 8 7 6 5 4 3 2 1

For David, my brother

Prologue

C**alico Dance had been at Prairie Books just two days when the first manuscript arrived. It came in a black envelope, addressed in typewritten capitals to Editorial Director Elizabeth McIntyre in person, but Calico quickly realized it wasn't really a personal letter. It was an unsolicited manuscript – Prairie Books received hundreds every day from would-be authors. There was a heap of them now on a table by Calico's desk, waiting to be read when someone had the time. It was called the slush pile.

Calico ought to have put this manuscript on the pile, but something about the covering letter caught her attention. It was typed, for a start, and, like the address, all in capitals. She'd read quite a few covering letters in her couple of days at the publishing house, but none like this. Generally they were either gushingly humble or politely matter-of-fact, but the tone of this was quite different:

DEAR MADAM, it read,

HERE IS THE FIRST INSTALMENT OF MY STORY, PUBLISH OR DIE! BE SURE YOU READ IT WELL. YOU, PERSONALLY. DON'T CHUCK THIS ON YOUR SLUSH PILE. READ, MARK, LEARN AND INWARDLY DIGEST. I HOLD YOU RESPONSIBLE.
REMEMBER: PUBLISH OR DIE.

The unmistakable air of menace contained in the letter was reflected in the name of its sender, a single word printed at the bottom: *NEMESIS*.

1

Calico knew nothing about publishing when she started at Prairie Books, beyond the obvious fact that it had something to do with books. And she certainly loved books; she had been an avid reader for as long as she could remember. She'd been at boarding school from the age of seven and there had always been lots of time for reading. Though a popular and active girl, in many ways books had been her best friends. So when, a week or so after leaving school, she was offered the job of editorial assistant at Prairie Books, she took it without hesitation. The post was to be just for the summer, but with the possibility of an indefinite extension depending on how things developed.

At present, Calico didn't know quite what she wanted. A career in publishing sounded glamorous, but she had other options to consider. She had a place waiting for her at university, but should she take it up this autumn or have a year out? Did she really want to go at all? Maybe she should just work long enough to save some money then follow in her parents' footsteps, go off travelling... Calico's parents had been professional travellers. They'd always been away on a trip somewhere and then been busy writing about it on their return. They'd compiled a whole library of guidebooks and journals and accounts of expeditions to deserts and jungles and remote islands. Growing up, Calico had seen her parents with increasing infrequency; if they weren't actually away from home, they were shut in their respective studies, working. Children just didn't fit in with their lifestyle, which is why Calico had been sent off to boarding school from an early age.

Others might have been resentful, but Calico wasn't. Her experiences had given her an independence of spirit that had made her well-liked and admired by her peers. She was the sort of person people readily got on with and confided in. She didn't think much about her own situation and wasted little time bemoaning it. She had, she knew, been a mistake. Her parents hadn't planned to have her, but they'd cared for her as best they could. Calico's real guardian and influence, though, had always been her Aunt Romy. Twice married but childless, Romy treated her brother's daughter as her own. It was she, not her parents, that Calico lived with during school holidays and she who could always be relied upon to make an appearance at sports and speech days. When Calico's parents were killed in an air crash over the Himalayas and, aged twelve, Calico became an orphan, Romy simply assumed officially the role that had always been hers.

It was Romy who had got Calico the job at Prairie Books. She was a respected and successful author of historical novels and knew Elizabeth McIntyre well. They'd met twelve years previously, when Elizabeth McIntyre was just starting out on her editorial career and had been assigned to work on one of Romy's books. Despite some initial disagreements, the pair had become friends and remained so after Elizabeth McIntyre moved to Prairie Books and in the years since. Hearing by chance that Elizabeth was in dire need of help after the sudden, acrimonious departure of her assistant, Romy had suggested Calico. Following a brief interview, at which she had impressed the formidable editor with her calm assurance, Calico had been offered the job.

Working at Prairie Books would be no doddle, though, Calico quickly discovered that. Elizabeth McIntyre had been called many things during her professional life, but easygoing was not one of them. Barely had Calico got in the door on her first day than her new boss was firing instructions at her. There were trays of correspondence to file, manuscripts to log in, people to phone – none of which fazed Calico one bit. What *did* concern her, however, was the early realization that Prairie Books was a company at war – with itself.

As Calico sifted through the mounds of letters and memos that first day, she became aware that a major power struggle was taking place. The principal players seemed to be Elizabeth McIntyre and her fellow editorial director, Austen Porter.

"You should see the way they talk to each other in their memos," she told her aunt. "I nearly got my fingers scorched just holding the paper."

Romy smiled. "Elizabeth can be pretty fiery," she agreed. "I don't really know Austen Porter, but I've heard he's a strong personality, too. He'd have to be to hold his own against Elizabeth." Her emerald eyes widened. "As I know well," she added. Calico nodded. Her aunt had told her a few stories about the clashes she'd had with Elizabeth McIntyre on that first book. At one point the then novice editor had threatened that if all her suggested changes weren't made then she wouldn't publish, upon which Romy had threatened to take the book elsewhere. Fortunately, they'd managed to sort out their differences and, in doing so, had become firm friends.

"It seems like Austen's got the support of the chairman, though," Calico said. Then, pulling a face, she declared, "*He's* a bit of a weird one, isn't he?"

Romy considered this for a moment. "Yes, I suppose so," she said at last. "Very charming, though. Very handsome, too – like his father."

"I find him a bit much," said Calico. She recalled

her brief meeting with the chairman that morning. She'd taken a memo from Elizabeth McIntyre up to his office. Immediately she entered his room, he'd got up from his desk, flashing her the warmest and most welcoming of smiles.

"You must be Calico," he had said and he'd shaken her hand. "You look very like your aunt. Just as beautiful." He spoke with a peculiar accent whose vowel sounds were a mixture of the twang of terribly-terribly English and the drawl of his native Georgia. His dress was indisputably English: neatly-pressed cream flannels, a white shirt with a green and yellow striped cricketer's tie and a camel-brown sleeveless sweater. His shoes were shiny brown brogues. Undeniably handsome, he was tall and very Anglo Saxon in looks with limpid blue eyes and neatly cut, fair hair. Calico found it hard to say how old he was – late thirties, forty maybe – but he had a boyish air about him that made her feel oddly mature.

"I'm sure it's going to be a pleasure having you with us," he had continued, beaming Calico another of his deeply appreciative smiles. "Do let me know if there's anything I can do for you while you're here."

"Yes, thank you," Calico had replied, somewhat overwhelmed by this show of genial hospitality. She'd found it quite flattering, too, until at lunch she'd witnessed him perform the same act to impress a visiting female author.

"Dale's problem," said Romy now, "is that he wasn't born English." Calico laughed. "He's a real

Anglophile," Romy went on. "You know, whenever I speak to him, I feel like I'm the foreigner. His charm certainly works, though. I know of some female authors who'd kill to be published on his list."

"Not you, though," Calico suggested.

"He's never asked me," Romy replied. Then she shook her head. "But no, not me." She had just delivered the manuscript for her fourteenth title to the company who'd first published her.

"I could always put in a good word for you," Calico offered, mischievously.

"Thank you, but I'm quite happy where I am," said Romy.

Anyone seeing aunt and niece together at that moment could not have helped but share P Dale Jefferson's opinion: there *was* a striking resemblance between them. They each had dark complexions with big, bright green eyes, high cheekbones and thick black, wavy hair. Romy's was cut short and threaded with grey, while Calico's hung in lustrous confusion halfway down her back and, at the front, spilled over her forehead, stopping just short of the single, deep chicken-pox scar that she had acquired in childhood. There was another similarity, too, less tangible but unmistakable nonetheless: a kind of open quality in both their faces that reflected their straightforward, unfussy natures.

Right now, though, Calico's face was a picture of alarm.

"I hope I'm not going to get caught in the

crossfire, if there's a war going on," she said, grimacing.

"Just keep your head down, dear," Romy advised. "Publishing's not the genteel world that people imagine. Dale may give the impression of being a bit of a fop, but underneath that suave, ever-so-English exterior, he's a tough cookie. He and Elizabeth have had some real fights."

"From what I read in those memos," said Calico, "it looks like there's another one on the way – with Austen Porter."

"Elizabeth doesn't pull her punches," Romy remarked, ruefully. "When she takes offence to something, her bite is every bit as bad as her bark." She nodded and opened her eyes wide. "Austen better beware. They'd *all* better beware…"

2

Elizabeth McIntyre was already in a meeting with Austen Porter and the chairman when Calico arrived at work the next morning. She'd written a note to say she probably wouldn't be around until lunch and left a list of tasks for Calico to complete. The first of these was opening the post, which is when she discovered the Nemesis letter and manuscript. She was reading the letter through for a third time, with some consternation, when Elizabeth McIntyre's right-hand editor, April Street, came by.

"Is everything OK?" April enquired, without real interest.

"Oh, yes," said Calico, distractedly. "It's just this." She handed the letter to April.

April glanced at the note without expression. As she watched April reading, it struck Calico that there was something almost android about her face. It was so passive. If you considered her features individually – small, well-formed mouth, largish deep-set grey eyes, strong nose and pale, smooth skin – they were actually quite impressive, but somehow the parts were more than the sum of the whole. There was something lacking; April had no spark. Everything about her was oddly dull and dowdy – from her mousy hair to her navy court shoes – almost as if she wanted to appear older than she really was. You'd never have guessed to look at her, in her long floral skirt and starchy white blouse with its high, restricting collar, that she was not yet thirty – six years younger than Elizabeth McIntyre. But she was, Romy had said. The two editors just had such amazingly different images. In her head, Calico pictured Elizabeth McIntyre with her bobbed, high-lighted hair, her striking make-up, designer jackets and short skirts, chosen to show off her fine legs…

"Nemesis," April muttered, contemptuously. "Revengeful justice." She passed the letter back to Calico. "I wouldn't worry," she said. "It's probably just a hoax. We do get some very peculiar letters, you know. People seem to think if they write something shocking then we'll be frightfully impressed and make them an offer on the spot."

"Oh," said Calico. She still wasn't convinced. "But shouldn't I show it to Ms McIntyre? It is rather threatening."

"Honestly, it's nothing to worry about, I'm sure,"

April said, with a smile that was barely more than a faint crease at the corners of her mouth. *Well, she should know*, Calico thought, as the editor walked away. April and Elizabeth McIntyre had worked together for several years.

Calico put the letter to one side and started on the rest of her tasks, the first of which was a call to an author's agent, Nina Mallinson, to rearrange an appointment Elizabeth McIntyre had made for that afternoon. Nina Mallinson was not amused.

"I'm a very busy woman," she barked down the phone with a voice like a weapon. "That appointment was made weeks ago – surely you could have let me know before now."

"I'm very sorry," Calico said politely, "I've only just joined Prairie Books. But I'm sure there's a very good reason why Ms McIntyre has had to cancel."

This remark was met by a "huh" of deep cynicism. "Elizabeth McIntyre does whatever she wants, whenever she wants," Nina Mallinson declaimed. "That's reason enough for her. Well, tell her that I shall be calling her later to rearrange our meeting. She can't keep Marvin hanging on like this. It isn't fair." The phone clicked and birred.

Marvin, Calico guessed, was Marvin Adams. His name had come up in the memos Calico had read and he seemed to be a major bone of contention: Elizabeth McIntyre thought a lot of him; Austen Porter didn't. Calico had never read any of Marvin Adams' books, but his last one, she knew, had caused quite a stir. Something about abortion and embryos, she recalled.

As it happened, her next task was to photocopy a manuscript by Marvin Adams: *Unholy Alliance*. It was a thick manuscript, over three hundred foolscap pages and would take ages to copy. Calico decided to take it down to the copier near the post-room behind reception. The machine there was quicker and gave better copies than the one in editorial, which, on long runs, grunted and squeaked like a pen full of piglets and drove the editors crazy. Besides, downstairs Calico could pack up some books to send out – another task on her list – while she did the photo-copying.

Joy Sparrow, the receptionist, greeted Calico with a cheery, "Hi, there," when she appeared in reception.

"Hi," Calico responded, warmly. Joy was the first person Calico had met at Prairie Books and she'd taken to her at once. When Calico had come for her interview with Elizabeth McIntyre, Joy had made her feel immediately at ease with her perky, friendly chat. A "resting actress" in her early twenties, Joy was blonde and chirpy and greeted everyone with a brilliant smile.

"Is that for photocopying?" she enquired now, nodding at the thick manuscript Calico was carrying.

"Yes," said Calico, pulling a wry expression.

"You can leave it with me, if you like. I'll put it on the machine later," said Joy. There was a beep and a light flashed on the switchboard before her. She motioned to Calico to wait and lifted the receiver.

"Good morning, Prairie Books," she chirped. No sooner had she put the call through to its intended party than another light flashed. Calico shook her head and quietly moved away. Joy had plenty of work to do, she thought, without taking on hers as well.

She put the opening five chapters on the machine and set it copying. Then, after waiting a moment or two to watch the first few pages come through, she went into the post-room.

"Uh-oh, it's an editor," the posty, Fred Brown, intoned gloomily, as if editors were the bane of his life. Calico had seen enough of Fred in the first couple of days to know that his remark wasn't meant personally. He met everyone with the same lugubrious air. With his saggy, heavily lined face, sunken eyes, prominent nose and huge rubbery ears, he reminded Calico of Eeyore in *Winnie-the-Pooh*.

"Don't worry, Fred," she said, breezily. "I've just come to get some books from the shed."

"Hmm," Fred mumbled, suspiciously. "I suppose you want me to get them for you."

"No," Calico smiled. "I can get them myself." Situated beneath the post-room, the shed was a large room of bookcases on which was stored a wide selection of Prairie Book titles. Dan Ryan, Fred's young assistant, had introduced Calico to it on her first day.

"Is Dan not in today?" she enquired now.

"I sent him down the post office," said Fred.

"Though why it's taken him so long to buy a few stamps I do not know." He frowned. "Young people, eh," he grumbled, assuming an expression of deep disenchantment. Calico turned away and grinned. She went to load another five chapters into the copier, then climbed down to the basement.

Calico really liked the shed. All those rows of pristine books, with their colourful spines, foil-blocked lettering – untouched, unopened, waiting to be read, like rows of potential friends waiting to make her acquaintance. One or two of them she'd met already – Elizabeth McIntyre had given her a couple of books to take away and read when she'd come for her interview – but most of them were exciting strangers. She'd been told she could help herself to a copy of anything she fancied and she couldn't wait to get started. The only question was, where to begin! She walked along the aisles now, collecting up the books she needed and enjoying the odd, almost monastic atmosphere of the place, before going back upstairs.

She put another block of pages in the copier, then walked into reception to talk to Joy. She found the receptionist facing the switchboard, looking unusually perplexed.

"What's up?" Calico asked.

Joy shook her head. "These people," she sighed. "They send in their manuscripts and they expect a reply just like that." She snapped her fingers together theatrically. "I explain to them that editors are very busy people and that we receive hundreds of unsolicited manuscripts every week. 'You'll get a response within two months,' I say. This guy just now said that wasn't good enough. He wanted me to assure him that Elizabeth McIntyre *personally* would read his manuscript. And when I said that I couldn't do that, he said, really icily, that I'd better make sure she did." She screwed up her face in displeasure. "You know, Calico, he really gave me the creeps."

"Sounds nasty," said Calico, with genuine sympathy. "Did he say who he was?"

"Yes," said Joy and she gave a slight involuntary shudder. "I'm not going to forget that in a hurry." She paused dramatically. "He called himself 'Nemesis'."

3

Elizabeth McIntyre's meeting with the chairman and Austen Porter lasted the best part of the day and it was late in the afternoon when she arrived back in her office. Seeing the look on her face, Calico was relieved that it was April she asked for first. Fortunately, half an hour in April's placid company seemed to cool her ire.

When Calico was finally summoned, she found Elizabeth McIntyre sitting at her round meeting table by the window with a distracted expression on her face. Calico gave her boss a quick progress report, but Elizabeth McIntyre's mind was not really there, she could tell. No doubt she was thinking about the events of *her* day.

"How did your meeting go?" Calico dared to ask.

Elizabeth McIntyre grimaced. "It was hell," she

pronounced. "Sheer bloody hell." She took a deep breath and sighed. "Do you smoke, Calico?" she asked.

"No," Calico said, surprised at the question.

"Good for you," Elizabeth McIntyre congratulated her. "I smoked for fifteen years and I'll always have the scars to prove it – bad teeth, lousy skin, tarred lungs." She screwed up her face in distaste. "I haven't smoked now for five years, but do you know, every time I go into a meeting with Dale and Austen I want to light up immediately. That's what those guys do to me." She coughed dryly. "I need a drink," she said.

She went over to a small fridge in the corner of the room and took out a bottle of white wine, which she put on the table with two glasses. Then she opened the top drawer of her desk and produced a corkscrew. With impressive adroitness, she quickly removed the cork from the bottle and poured two glasses of wine.

"You do drink wine, don't you?" she asked rather belatedly.

"A little," said Calico. In truth, she didn't drink. She didn't like the taste of alcohol. But she thought to say so would sound childish and she didn't want Ms McIntyre to think of her as a child. She'd only known the editor for a couple of days but already she had an enormous respect for her. She wanted her approval.

Elizabeth McIntyre raised her glass. "Cheers," she said and drank deeply.

Calico, by contrast, took a small sip. When she put down her glass, Elizabeth McIntyre was eyeing her keenly.

"Now, Calico," she said. "I'm going to tell you a story."

The story Elizabeth McIntyre told was basically the history of Prairie Books and her own part in it, fleshing out what Calico already knew. Dale Jefferson Senior had established the company as a publisher of "thumping good reads" – the kind of popular, accessible fiction that Elizabeth McIntyre herself liked. So, when Dale Jefferson offered her a job, she had no hesitation in accepting. Within a year and still only twenty-six, she had risen to the post of editorial director. Over the next seven years, Elizabeth McIntyre and Prairie Books had gone from strength to strength. Then, two years ago, Dale Jefferson Senior had died suddenly of a heart attack and his son had taken over.

At this point, Elizabeth McIntyre poured herself another glass of wine.

"That's when the problems started," she said bitterly. "Dale Junior's not like his father. He's really not interested in *books*, he's interested in *prizes*. He thinks we should be publishing great works of English literature that will bring him glory." She paused and her eyes hardened into steel. "Anyway, a year ago Dale brought in Austen to realize his literary dream. Well, I had no quarrel with that. I thought our lists would complement one another. Little did I realize Austen's ambition was to push me out." She took another large sip of wine.

The meeting that afternoon, she went on to tell Calico, had been very unpleasant. She'd almost felt like resigning there and then. Austen had launched a scathing attack on Marvin Adams and his new manuscript, *Unholy Alliance*. It was tasteless, sensationalist rubbish, he said, just like Adams' last book, *The Embryo Clinic*, and it was time they stopped publishing such trash. As she reported this, Elizabeth McIntyre seemed visibly to smoulder.

"Stuffy, arrogant prig," she hissed. "The book sold like hot cakes, I told them. It was a roaring success. 'But what an awful upset it caused,' Dale blathered. 'We have a reputation to uphold.' 'Yes,' I agreed. 'A reputation for making books that people want to read.' Then he gave me that smarmy look of his. 'But not at any cost, Elizabeth,' he said. 'And this time, the moral cost is just too great.' So that's it. Marvin Adams must go — for the sake of a few hysterical anti-abortionists." Elizabeth McIntyre looked into her empty glass like it was an old friend that had sorely disappointed her.

"Do you know, Calico," she sighed. "I'd like to put a bomb up that man sometimes." This image seemed to restore her good humour and she chuckled to herself momentarily. Then she looked at Calico with eyes that struggled to focus clearly.

"Anyway, I ought to let you go home," she said,

eventually. "I've kept you too long. Why don't you order us a cab and I'll drop you off? You'll find the number in my address book under 'C'."

"OK. Thanks," Calico said, grateful for the offer; it had been a long, eventful day. She got up and went over to the desk.

"Tomorrow is another day," said Elizabeth McIntyre, with weary irony. "And it can't be any worse than today, can it?"

"I guess not," Calico agreed, with a sympathetic smile.

But, as it turned out, they were wrong.

4

At 8.46 the following morning, while Calico was standing on a packed bus on her way to work, a letter bomb exploded in the reception of Prairie Books. Fortunately for Joy Sparrow, who opened it, the explosive was an incendiary device, not a real bomb, or her injuries would have been much more serious than the minor burns and shock that she suffered.

As Calico arrived at Prairie Books, she was dismayed to see Joy being helped into an ambulance and bewildered at the sight of the three fire engines and two police cars parked in front of the building. When she learned what had happened she, like her fellow employees, was utterly horrified. Who on earth would do such a thing?

The police remained at the publishing house for

most of the morning, conducting interviews and inquiries. They gave the impression that they believed the bomb to be the work of PUC (Protectors of the Unborn Child), the extremist pro-life group who had issued threats against Prairie Books after the publishing of Marvin Adams' *The Embryo Clinic*.

Calico spent the morning covering for Joy. The reception area had sustained only minor damage and the telephone switchboard was still functioning normally. In fact, the lines were busier than ever with the press joining the usual publishing business calls. Calico put several calls through to the press office. She had three requests, too, for copies of the controversial Adams book. She was dealing with the third one when Judy Price, the production director, walked into reception.

"I wish we'd never published the damn thing," she muttered when Calico came off the line. "It's a silly book and it's caused nothing but trouble. It was a waste of good paper. I told Elizabeth so at the time." A nervy woman who rarely smiled, today Judy Price looked even more on edge. Like Austen Porter and Dale Jefferson, she was a heavy smoker and looked lost without a cigarette in her hand. She chewed at her lips anxiously, her pallid face twitchy with strain.

"At least that's the last that we'll be publishing of the wretched man's books," she added with tart satisfaction, before depositing a parcel for collection and departing. When it came to Marvin Adams, clearly Judy Price was in the Porter camp.

It was time, Calico decided, that she read *The Embryo Clinic*; everyone seemed to be talking about it. And, moreover, she was going to meet the author later: he was coming in with Nina Mallinson for the rearranged meeting with Elizabeth McIntyre.

It was lunchtime before a temp arrived to relieve Calico. Then she went down to the shed to pick up a copy of Marvin Adams' controversial book. As Joy wasn't around – nor Dan either, it seemed – and it was such a warm, bright day, Calico thought she'd spend her lunch hour outside reading. There was a small courtyard at the back of Prairie Books and she sat on a bench there to make a start on *The Embryo Clinic*...

When she next looked at her watch, it was five to two and she'd raced through the first six chapters. What's more, she'd thoroughly enjoyed them. Adams had a simple, punchy style with lots of dialogue that moved the story along at a breathless pace. OK, she could see that it wasn't classic fiction, but no way could she go along with Judy Price's opinion that it was a waste of paper. And nor was it offensive. *The Embryo Clinic* was just a brilliant read – a rattling good story – and she couldn't wait to read more. That, surely, was the sign of a really good book. Yep, on the subject of Marvin Adams, Calico was in total sympathy with Elizabeth McIntyre. She felt a tingle of excitement that she was actually going to meet the author later. That was one of the things that had really attracted her to the job in editorial –

the prospect of meeting authors. Now, though, it was time to get back to work.

The first thing that caught her eye when she sat down at her desk was the Nemesis manuscript. She gazed at it for a second or two with a slightly puzzled air. It wasn't on the pile of unsolicited manuscripts where she thought she had put it, but over the other side of the desk, on top of the Marvin Adams manuscript she had photocopied the previous day. Someone must have moved it.

She picked up the letter, noticing for the first time that the sender's address was a box number, Box No. 111. Then remembering the call Joy had received the day before, she felt a flash of annoyance. People who played stupid mystery games like that should be told where to get off. They shouldn't be allowed to get away with making threats and upsetting people. It was really pathetic and irresponsible. What right did this Nemesis have to write offensive stuff like that and then hide behind some box number?

She picked up the manuscript that had accompanied the letter and, for the first time, started to read it properly, hoping that she'd find lots to criticize and ridicule in the stinging reply she intended to send. It wasn't a complete story, just "the first instalment", as the letter had announced (rather self-importantly, Calico thought).

The story was called *Publish or Die*, and it concerned a woman who wrote a story that she believed to be a potential bestseller. She sent it to a publishing company, who, to her delight, shared her belief. They wanted to publish and offered her a big advance. A lucrative three-book contract was proposed. The woman was fêted and treated like a star. Then, suddenly, everything changed. A new editorial director arrived at the publishing house and at her insistence the offer was withdrawn. She didn't like the book, she said. A letter of rejection was sent and plans for publication were abandoned. The woman was bewildered and angry. How could they go back on their word? She sent letters – at first cajoling, then threatening – demanding that her book be published as promised. The company replied that no contract had been drawn up, there was no obligation. After that, they simply ignored her altogether. Now the woman was really mad. She wanted revenge. She decided to begin a campaign of terror…

Calico turned the page. As she read on, a frown formed on her face, for the actions described had an uncomfortable familiarity. Furious at the lack of response to her demand, the woman sent a letter bomb. It exploded in the company's reception area, causing major damage and maiming the glamorous receptionist, for whom, apparently, the woman had a particular aversion. Calico put down the manuscript.

It was just a coincidence, of course, but it was an unhappy one, bringing back all too vividly what had occurred at Prairie Books earlier in the day. How *was* Joy? Calico wondered now, starting to feel angry all over again on behalf of the injured receptionist towards the pro-life extremists responsible, it seemed, for sending the letter bomb.

A man's voice interrupted her reverie. "Wow, that must be a real stinker."

Calico looked up to see Dan Ryan smiling down at her. She took in his short, strawberry-blond hair, wide, generous mouth and eyes that were a liquid turquoise in the sunlight. She returned his smile tentatively.

"You were giving that paper a really murderous look," Dan continued.

Calico raised her eyes. "Ah, it's nothing, rubbish really," she said. "It's just that... Well, here, see for yourself."

She handed Dan the letter and the manuscript. He shrugged. "I'm no editor," he said. He spoke with a slight accent that Calico couldn't place. A trace of Irish, perhaps, or was it American? Well, it was very attractive, whatever it was.

"You don't need to be," said Calico. Then she nodded at the papers in his hand. "Have a read," she prompted. "See what you think."

"OK," he agreed, pleasantly.

He read the letter and pulled a face. "Weird," he said.

"Read on," Calico urged.

She watched him as he read the manuscript. His fair, bright complexion was a supernova of expressive freckles, giving his face an impression of natural affability that, being instinctively friendly herself,

Calico found very appealing.

The half-hour she'd spent with Dan down in the shed on her first afternoon had been the most agreeable of her time at Prairie Books so far. They'd talked to one another with open ease – about their lives, how they came to be at Prairie Books, what they intended to do in the future... He'd arrived about three months ago from university, where he'd spent a year studying English literature. He'd decided, he'd said, to take an indefinite time-out while he considered what he really wanted to do. He was most interested in plays – Elizabethan and Jacobean drama especially – and there wasn't enough of that on his course. It was all boring novels, he'd remarked, with a wry nod at the shed's packed shelves.

He had a similar amused air as he looked up from reading now.

"It's a bit far-fetched, isn't it?" he said. "I can't say I'm dying to read the next instalment."

"But what about the explosion bit?" Calico enquired. His eyes narrowed in comprehension. "Ah, yes," he said. "You mean it's like what happened here this morning."

Calico nodded. Then she told him about the Nemesis phone call that Joy had taken.

"Sounds like a bit of a sicko," Dan said. "But I doubt it's anything to worry about." He wrinkled his nose, setting off a kind of starburst of freckles. "Joy's OK, by the way. She phoned from the hospital. She says she'll be back tomorrow. And as for this," he held up the manuscript with a contemptuous expression, "well, it's not exactly an original plot, is it? I'd not be surprised if you'd find a fair few like it in that big pile you've got there." He nodded with a wry smile at the slush pile.

Calico sighed and grinned. The good news about Joy had lifted an unconscious weight from her shoulders.

"You're right," she said decisively. "Thanks, Dan. I'll send the thing back this afternoon with the biting rejection it deserves."

"Good on you," said Dan. He stood in thought for a moment, then, with a soft laugh, added, "Give Nemesis his nemesis. There's a poetic justice about that."

"If you say so," Calico agreed, sharing his amusement. "Anyway, hopefully that's the last we'll hear of him."

As she was soon to discover, however, Nemesis was not to be so easily dismissed.

5

When Calico got home that evening, Romy was just packing up work for the day. She set herself a strict regime, working most days from nine until seven with a short break for lunch. She had no agent, so she had her business affairs to sort out as well as her writing, and then there was always plenty of post to answer. Romy was a prolific letter writer (something that Calico had greatly appreciated when at school; Romy's regular letters being a highlight of each week) and she replied to every letter received. She kept most of them, too, in a big oak wardrobe in her bedroom.

Having been in her study all day, Romy hadn't heard the news and when Calico told her about the letter bomb she was deeply shocked. She poured herself a large dry sherry and made Calico sit down and tell her in detail about what had happened. Calico told her aunt about the bomb and Joy going to hospital and the line of inquiry the police were taking.

Talk of the police inquiries led on to the subject of Marvin Adams. After her eager anticipation earlier at meeting the author, the reality had been something of a let-down.

"He wasn't at all what I expected," Calico said, recalling the author's drooping, lined face, his small, doleful eyes and the odd wreath-like arrangement of gingery-grey hair that adorned his head. He looked, Calico thought, like a man for whom even the most trivial matter would be a cause for concern. Standing there in the reception of Prairie Books, he appeared positively suicidal.

"What *did* you expect?" Romy asked, lightly.

"Oh, I don't know," said Calico. "Someone younger, I guess. More sort of suave, sexy. Scary even."

"Oh, Marvin Adams can be scary when he wants to be," Romy said. "And violent, too. He killed someone once, you know."

"Marvin Adams killed someone?" Calico questioned, incredulously.

Romy nodded. "He stabbed some chap in an argument," she said. "Got off on self-defence, as I recall."

"Wow," Calico muttered, shocked. She couldn't imagine that cowed bear of a man raising his voice, never mind killing someone.

"He's a very introverted man, apparently, and very unpredictable," Romy continued. "One moment he might be mild as milk, the next throwing a violent tantrum. I don't envy Nina Mallinson her job at all."

"No," Calico agreed. "Though I'm sure if anyone can handle him, she can. She's a real dragon, isn't she?"

She pictured Nina Mallinson in her mind's eye: a small, fierce woman with iron-grey hair and a voice that could cut through steel. The word *waspish* could have been coined just for her. She'd given Calico a real tongue-lashing as they'd made their way to Ms McIntyre's office. It had been quite a relief to get away. "I wonder how she and Ms McIntyre got on."

Romy smiled broadly. "Sparks flew, I imagine," she said, mischievously. "No doubt you'll hear all about it tomorrow."

"I hope so," Calico said lightly, responding in kind to her aunt's playful tone.

Elizabeth McIntyre was usually one of the first to arrive at Prairie Books in the morning, but when Calico arrived next day, the editor's office was empty.

Joy was back, though. She greeted Calico with her customary smile and a newly bandaged hand. A few minor burns, she said, were the full extent of her injuries and she didn't see any point in staying at home even though Dale Jefferson had given her leave to do so.

"I've had quite enough of 'resting'," she said, with

an ironic reference to her acting career. "Besides," she added, flashing Calico a glorious smile as she handed her a small pile of mail, "what would you do without me?"

"Too right," Calico agreed. She'd been at Prairie Books long enough to realize the high esteem in which Joy was held and how much people relied upon her. If she ever got another acting job, she thought, she'd be a very hard act to follow!

Up at her desk, Calico made herself a cup of coffee then settled down to deal with the post. By ten o'clock, she'd finished and there was still no sign of Ms McIntyre. Perhaps she had an appointment that she'd forgotten to tell Calico about or maybe something had come up after Calico had left the evening before. The best thing to do, Calico decided, would be to take a glance at the editor's diary that she always left open on her desk. Calico looked but there was nothing marked there.

When she turned towards the doorway, Austen Porter was there. He was dressed as usual in khaki canvas trousers, denim jacket and a black T-shirt, at the neck of which a multicoloured silk neckerchief flourished surprisingly.

"Her majesty not in yet, then?" he enquired with a sneer.

Calico frowned. "Do you mean Ms McIntyre?" she asked, with exaggerated innocence. She knew perfectly well who Austen Porter was referring to.

"Yes, *Ms* McIntyre," Austen Porter said, with

mock respect. Mockery was an expression that sat easily on his thin, pale face. He had dark receding hair, little piggy eyes, a long aqualine nose and skinny lips. His natural expression was one of sneering intolerance and the impression he gave Calico, as she observed him now, was of someone whose love for his fellow beings was as thin as his face.

"No," she said, "Ms McIntyre's not in yet."

"Well, when is she coming in?" Austen Porter persisted.

"I don't know," said Calico, refusing to be bullied. "She hasn't got any appointments this morning and she did have a very difficult meeting yesterday afternoon..." She shrugged. "I'm sure she'll be in soon."

"Well, that's very reassuring," Austen Porter remarked sourly. His sneer grew more pronounced. "Perhaps you'd be so kind as to ask her to call me when she does make an appearance. We have things to discuss."

"Certainly," Calico said, with cool politeness, though inside she was seething. No wonder Elizabeth McIntyre disliked this man so much. Calico had never met anyone so unpleasant.

Half an hour passed and there was still no word from Ms McIntyre. Calico phoned down to Joy to ask if her boss had left any message.

"No," said Joy. "I've heard nothing. She usually says when she's going to be in late."

"I wonder where she is," Calico pondered.

"She couldn't be at a book club or somewhere with Judy Price, could she?" Joy suggested. "Only Judy's not in this morning either and no one seems to know where she is." Then, "Austen's fuming," she added, in a melodramatic stage whisper.

"Don't I know," said Calico, with a conspiratorial laugh. "I'll ask April, she'll probably know. I'll catch you later, Joy." She was about to remove the receiver from her ear when Joy's breathy cry stopped her.

"Hold on a mo," she said. "I've got a delivery for you. Dan's going to bring it up."

"A delivery?" Calico queried. "What sort of delivery?" She was still new enough in the job to find an unscheduled delivery mildly intriguing.

"Oh, just a letter for Elizabeth, nothing very exciting," Joy laughed. "Well, unless," she went on, "you find black envelopes exciting."

6

The letter was from Nemesis, Calico was sure of that. It bore all the hallmarks: the black envelope with a small white label, addressed in typed capitals to Elizabeth McIntyre. Yet Calico had only sent her rejection yesterday afternoon – second class too, so it couldn't have arrived yet…

Intrigued in spite of herself, Calico tore open the envelope and removed the papers inside. As before, there was a letter and a manuscript; as before, the letter bore a box number and was typed in capitals.

DEAR MADAM, it read,

HERE IS THE SECOND INSTALMENT OF MY STORY, PUBLISH OR DIE! IGNORE OR REJECT IT AT YOUR PERIL. THE ETERNAL

EYE SEES THROUGH ALL. ON YOUR HEAD
BE IT.
  REMEMBER: PUBLISH OR DIE.
  NEMESIS.

Apart from the reference to "the eternal eye" this
second letter was much the same as the first. Its tone
was just as chilly and menacing. This time, though,
it had much less effect. Since her discussion with
Dan, Calico had come to view Nemesis as a sad,
inadequate attention-seeker, the letter writing
equivalent of a park flasher and she was no longer
intimidated. Besides, she had no time to pay the
letter any further mind because at that moment
Elizabeth McIntyre strode into the department.

"Morning, Calico," she said, with unexpected
heartiness.

"Good morning, Ms McIntyre," Calico responded. She followed the editor into her office.

"I'd love a cup of coffee, Calico," said Elizabeth
McIntyre, as she settled herself behind her desk. She
looked great, Calico thought, as she went out into the
department again, really stunning. Her make-up was
as immaculate as ever and she was wearing large
silver leaf earrings, a striking burnt amber silk blouse
and an elegant black skirt.

Calico poured a cup of the tarry-black liquid that
smelt unpleasantly stewed, but she knew that her
boss wouldn't care; if anything she seemed to prefer
it that way.

"Ah, thanks, Calico," Elizabeth McIntyre cooed when Calico put the steaming mug down on the desk before her.

"I'm sorry I'm late," she added airily. "I had a couple of things to sort out this morning. Any messages?"

Calico nodded. "Just one," she said. "Austen Porter wants to see you." Even as she spoke, she was preparing herself for an adverse reaction; if there was anything guaranteed to ruin Elizabeth McIntyre's good humour, it was, surely, the mention of Austen Porter. But this morning, apparently, the editor's high spirits were quite unsinkable. She grinned, the picture of style and contentment.

"Uh-huh," she said, archly. "Well, as it happens, I want to see him, too."

Something was afoot, Calico was sure. But she hadn't a clue what it could be. She'd expected her boss to be a little downhearted after the difficult meeting with Marvin Adams and his agent the evening before. Yet here she was, chirpy as anything. Had the meeting gone much better than anticipated? What could have happened? Calico was dying to know, but she had little time to ponder these questions because at that moment the fire alarm went off. The noise was deafening: an insistent, piercingly high-pitched wail that sent Calico's hands flying to her ears. In seconds, people were moving in the department around her, making their way towards the exit. Elizabeth McIntyre appeared in her office doorway. Calico looked at her questioningly.

"Go along with the others, Calico," the editor instructed. "They'll show you what to do." She herself showed no signs of going anywhere. She was extraordinarily calm and composed.

"But what about you, Ms McIntyre?" Calico asked.

"Oh, I'm the fire officer," said the editor, jovially. "I've just got to check this floor, then I'll be down."

Calico nodded, then she walked off after the others.

They collected in the small square opposite the building. April Street had a list of all the names in the editorial department and, with calm impassivity, she called them out, then ticked them off one by one as they answered her call. Designated staff in other departments did the same. Meanwhile, for the second morning in a row, three fire engines arrived, lights flashing, sirens shrieking and soon the street outside Prairie Books was busy with firemen.

At first, no one seemed to know whether there really was a fire or not, but after what had happened the day before, the mood was uneasy. And the tension intensified when the firemen started to unroll one of the heavy hoses. Calico was observing intently with everyone else when Joy came over.

"What's happening?" Calico asked.

"It seems there's a fire in the basement," Joy informed her. "Fred saw smoke and he set off the alarm."

"Is it serious?" Calico enquired.

Joy shrugged and sighed. "I really don't know," she admitted.

"I hope not."

It was a hope shared by everyone standing there and watching as the firemen went into action.

It was only then that Calico realized that her boss was missing. She turned to Joy. "Have you seen, Ms McIntyre?" she asked.

"No," Joy said. She glanced around. "Didn't she come out with the rest of you?"

Calico shook her head and told Joy of the conversation she'd had with Ms McIntyre upstairs.

Joy frowned, her bright eyes unusually sombre. "I was the last one to leave," she said. "And I don't remember seeing her come out."

"I'd better tell April," said Calico, decisively.

Calico's news brought a rare spark to April Street's grey eyes. They flickered briefly with surprise and something else – irritation, Calico thought.

"Oh, is Elizabeth in?" she said. "I didn't know."

"She'd just arrived," Calico informed her. Then she related once more the last thing Elizabeth McIntyre had said.

"But I was the last to leave the department," said April coolly. "Are you sure Elizabeth was there?"

"Yes," said Calico, with some impatience. "I had a conversation with her."

"Oh, well," said April dully, her hand going to the brooch at her throat as if to turn off communication, "she must be around here somewhere." And that was that, it seemed, as far as April Street was concerned. Her face set back into its android mask and evidently she had no intention of taking the matter any further. But Calico wasn't satisfied. There was a fire in the building and for all anybody knew, Elizabeth McIntyre could still be in there.

"I'm going to speak to the firemen," she told Joy.

"OK, I'll come with you," the receptionist offered.

On their way through the crowd, they met Dan.

"What's up?" he enquired, pleasantly. They explained and his eyes, a deep green in the sunlight, narrowed in a frown.

"You were one of the last to leave, Dan. Did you see her?" Joy asked.

Dan shook his blond head. "Not that I recall," he said. "She might have gone out the back, I suppose." This suggestion of an alternative exit reassured Calico a little, but still she decided to alert the firemen.

The fireman they approached didn't want to speak to them at first. He scowled and, raising a burly arm, tried to send them back to the others. But Calico's persistence made him listen.

"All right, love," he said when he'd heard her out, "we'll check it out, don't worry. The fire's all down in the basement so she can't be in any danger. We've got it under control."

The comforting effect of these words was spoiled almost at once, however, when a young fireman rushed out of the building, requesting an ambulance to be called.

"What's up, Jack?" the burly fireman asked.

"We found someone down there, Pete," Jack replied. "A woman."

Calico's heart stopped, then started to race away like a sprinter from the gun.

"A w-woman," she stuttered. "Is she OK?"

The young fireman's expression lacked the composure of his older colleague.

"I don't know," he said. "They're bringing her out now."

A couple of moments later, Elizabeth McIntyre appeared, arms over the shoulders of two large firemen as they lifted her limp body out on to the pavement. Gently they sat her down and she slumped forward. At once, Calico and Joy were at her side. Dan ran over, too.

"Are you all right, Ms McIntyre?" Calico asked, anxiously.

Elizabeth McIntyre looked up groggily and blinked several times. Her face was flushed from the heat of the fire and smudged with soot; her clothes were rumpled. It was hard to recognize the elegant, buoyant editor Calico had left barely twenty minutes before. Her eyes moved from one to the other of the three worried faces staring down at her as if trying to focus, then, at last, they settled on Calico. She took a deep breath, closed her eyes and sighed. Her lips rose slightly in a faint smile.

"Yes, I'm all right," she said, hoarsely. "I'm all right."

Then she slumped forward once more.

7

Elizabeth McIntyre would not go to hospital. Sitting on a sofa in reception, she quickly recovered herself and, in typically forthright fashion, dismissed all expressions of concern from the group gathered around her. She was fine, she said. Her throat was a little raw from the smoke she'd inhaled, but then, she remarked, this was a minor irritant for someone who'd smoked heavily for fifteen years of her life. A short toilet break and, with the exception of the odd wrinkle in her clothes, she emerged once again as the immaculately groomed, stylish and highly prepossessing editor that everyone was used to.

Calico was amazed, almost awestruck, at the transformation. After all, as the fire chief noted, a little longer in that smoky basement and Elizabeth

McIntyre would almost certainly have died. This chilly thought made Calico grimace but appeared to have little effect on Ms McIntyre. When she thanked the firemen for delivering her from the fumes, it was with genuine yet casual appreciation, as if they had just rescued her cat from a tree.

The shed had been badly damaged by the fire and most of its contents destroyed. While the firemen cleared up and searched for clues as to what had started the blaze, Elizabeth McIntyre tried to recall what had happened. She remembered, she said, inspecting her department when all the others had left. She checked that all the doors and windows were closed. Then she went back into her own room to get her bag. The burly fireman tutted heavily at this.

"You should have gone straight downstairs," he reprimanded her. "Bags can be replaced, lives can't."

"Not *my* bag," Ms McIntyre countered sharply, proving beyond all doubt that she was back to her fighting self. "My bag *is* my life." The fireman just puckered his lips and shook his head censoriously.

"But how on earth did you end up in the basement, Elizabeth?" April Street enquired with the same edge of irritation that Calico had heard in her voice out on the street. In that atmosphere of friendly concern it struck an oddly inappropriate note, Calico thought. She hadn't taken to April from the moment she'd met her and the morning's incidents had only confirmed her dislike.

"I'm not entirely sure," Elizabeth McIntyre continued muzzily. "I remember coming down to reception and seeing it empty."

"I must have just left," Joy offered. "I was the last, except for Fred – and Dan, maybe?"

Fred nodded his large head sombrely. His big, heavy features had set into an expression of profound gloom that made him appear even more like Eeyore than usual. "I was last out," he pronounced.

"Perhaps you saw smoke coming from the post-room?" suggested Ruth Davies, one of the desk editors.

Elizabeth McIntyre frowned as if in deep concentration. Then her eyes regained their keenness. "No, no," she muttered. "It wasn't smoke I saw. It was a person. I saw someone in the post-room."

"Fred?" Joy prompted.

Elizabeth McIntyre shook her head. "No, not Fred," she said. "At least…"

"Who then?" April demanded.

"I don't know," Elizabeth McIntyre admitted with a sigh. "It was so quick, just a glimpse. Maybe there was no one there at all. I just remember thinking there was. So I went to look. I thought I ought to." She smiled ironically. "I am a fire officer, after all."

The burly fireman shook his head again. "That's very commendable, madam," he said, "but you should leave the heroics to us. We're better equipped."

Elizabeth McIntyre gave a dismissive flick of her head. "Don't worry, I wasn't intending to do anything heroic," she said. "I just thought I ought to investigate, that's all. If I'd encountered any danger, I'd have been out of there like a bat out of hell, I can tell you."

"You did end up in the danger area, though," the fireman pointed out.

"Yes, yes, I did, didn't I?" Elizabeth McIntyre conceded. "I thought that's where the person must have gone."

"But you didn't know then that that's where the fire was," Calico said, coming to her boss's defence. "None of us did, except Fred and Joy – and Dan, I suppose."

"Yes, that's right," chirped Joy. "So you didn't know you were going into danger."

"No," Ms McIntyre agreed. "And by the time I found out it was too late." She grimaced. "The smoke was terrible. I couldn't see anything. And I couldn't breathe."

"You were very lucky," said the fireman, with obvious admiration.

April, however, was not so impressed. "I'm surprised you couldn't get out, Elizabeth," she said sharply, with the tone of a school matron who suspected a sick child of malingering. "Surely, the smoke couldn't have overwhelmed you that quickly."

This accusatory suggestion made Calico's hackles rise, but Elizabeth McIntyre simply shrugged.

"I did try to get out," she said. "I remember turning and making for the door. But it wouldn't open.

Or maybe that's when the smoke got to me."

"Could the door have been locked?" Joy asked Fred, who met the suggestion with a look of deep affront.

"I never locked it," he said. "I could ask Dan..." Dan was downstairs, assisting the firemen.

"No need," said the burly fireman. "That's a heavy fire door. My men could never have got in so fast if they'd had to break it down. The door wasn't locked." He gave Elizabeth McIntyre a pinched smile. "Fortunately for you, madam."

"Yes," she agreed. "Lucky me."

At that moment, Dan appeared, a grim-faced young fireman in tow.

"They think they've found the cause," Dan announced, and at once all eyes turned towards him.

"This," said the young fireman, holding up a cigarette stub. "It was right where the fire started."

The older fireman shook his head. "Smokers," he said, disgustedly. "They're a menace."

"You're right there," Elizabeth McIntyre concurred, though not, Calico suspected, for the same reason. "I've suggested a number of times that this should be a non-smoking building. But when the chairman's the main culprit, well..." She shrugged. "Still, that's all going to change," she added mysteriously and Calico saw once more the strange, almost triumphant gleam that had been in her eye when she'd arrived that morning. Evidently she knew something to her advantage, but what could it be? Calico wondered. Elizabeth McIntyre's voice cut short her speculation.

"And now," said the renowned editor, getting up from the sofa with a purposeful air, "I think it's time we all got back to work."

8

"Oh, wow," Calico exclaimed in awestruck tones as she studied the burnt-out mess that had been the Prairie Books shed. She'd come down with Dan to take a look at "devastation row", as he referred to it. And now she could see why. The whitewashed walls were grey with charcoal and there was ash scattered all over the room. The shelves that had been so resplendent with pristine volumes were now piled with cinder leaves. To Calico, for whom books were a kind of treasure – something beautiful, precious, almost sacred – the sight was deeply affecting. "All those books, all those words," she said, sombrely.

"There's plenty more where they came from," Dan remarked, drily. "There's too many novels in the world anyway."

"Dan!" Calico rebuked. "How could you say that?"

"It's true," he said. Then he grinned sheepishly. "I told you, I'm into plays."

"Yes, but even so," said Calico. "It's such a waste." She took a step across the crisp black floor and rescued a book from one of the shelves. It was one of the very few volumes that were still intact after the fire, though the bottom corner of the right-hand pages had been singed away and there were yellowy-brown scorch marks across the dust jacket. Calico wiped it clean of ash and inspected it.

"Hey!" she cried. "It's a Marvin Adams. *The Embryo Clinic*."

"There's an irony," Dan commented. "There are those pro-life people demanding the book be burnt and it's the only one to survive the fire. Weird." He prodded at another charred volume with his foot. "It'll take a while to clear this lot up," he said.

At that instant, he looked so melancholy and vulnerable that Calico felt like hugging him. And she might have, if she'd known him a little better. As it was she contented herself with some gentle cajoling.

"Cheer up," she said. "Just think of all that verbal garbage you'll be disposing of." He turned and looked at her and she was struck once more by the extraordinary chameleon-quality of his eyes that now, in the basement gloom, appeared almost grey. She had never seen eyes like Dan's before.

"The first thing I'm going to do is put up a big

no–smoking sign," he said. Then he smiled broadly. "Fred's orders."

"I bet he's furious," said Calico, who knew even from the short time that she had been at Prairie Books, how jealously Fred guarded his area of the building. "He'll probably be demanding an inquest."

"I doubt whether the chairman would go along with that," said Dan. When Calico looked at him quizzically, he continued, "Well, he'd be one of the prime suspects, wouldn't he, being such a heavy smoker?"

"I suppose," said Calico and it started her thinking. "I wonder who *was* responsible," she said. "Someone must know it was them, mustn't they?" She frowned. "I'd have to say if it was me, wouldn't you?"

Dan considered this briefly. "Well, yes," he said, doubtfully. "But I suppose it might be different if you had an important job and it was like on the line, you know."

"No," said Calico. "That wouldn't make any difference. Not to me. I'd have to say, whatever."

Dan appraised her wryly. "You know, you'd make a good tragic heroine," he said.

"I'll take that as a compliment," she replied heartily, returning his smile, and hoping that there was as much warmth in it as there was in her own.

Going back upstairs to her desk, Calico ran into Austen Porter and his assistant, Mitch Lennon.

"So, we meet again," said the older man. "Has

Madam recovered from her ordeal?" The tone of this enquiry was, it seemed to Calico, just about as graceless and uncaring as could be. Behind Austen, Mitch grinned horsily.

"Ms McIntyre's fine," Calico said.

"Good," said Austen, "because I'm on my way to see her and I wouldn't like to have to hold back at all out of pity."

"Don't worry," Calico rejoined, inwardly amused at the preposterous notion of Austen Porter showing anyone pity, "Ms McIntyre's quite ready for you."

They walked the rest of the way to Elizabeth McIntyre's office in hostile silence.

While Austen Porter went in to talk to his fellow editorial director, Mitch Lennon followed Calico to her desk. He stood over her, leering, for a moment or two.

"Well, Calico," he said at last. "We haven't met, have we?"

"No," she said.

"I'm Mitch," he announced, as if he were offering her some highly desirable gift. "But then I expect you know that already."

"Yes," she replied. "You work for Mr Porter."

"Austen," he corrected her. "Yeah. We're a team." There was something so absurdly grandiose about this statement that Calico almost laughed. After all, Mitch could hardly be much older than she was and she knew his position in the company, like hers, was very junior indeed. The way he spoke, though, you'd have thought he and Austen Porter were equals.

"I guess it must be a bit tough for you," Mitch continued, "working for a dragon like Elizabeth Mac." His fleshy lips drew back to reveal his horsy, big-toothed grin. "She's on her way out, you know," he confided, knowingly.

"Really?" said Calico.

Mitch nodded, his bony face disappearing momentarily behind a lank veil of hair. "Yeah. It's time for youth to have its day, eh?" he added conspiratorially.

Calico smiled despite herself and shook her head. "I don't think Elizabeth McIntyre's going anywhere," she stated confidently.

"No?" said Mitch and he gave her an arch look. "We'll see."

And with this, he slid away in the direction of April Street.

Calico turned her attention once more to the steadily mounting slush pile, on top of which was the second Nemesis offering. She picked up the black envelope and opened it, registering again the letter with its curious reference to the "eternal eye" and then moving on to the manuscript itself. This time, she determined, she'd give it no more than a cursory glance: Nemesis had taken up far too much of her time already this first week.

Publish or Die continued much as it had begun with the aggrieved woman author swearing vengeance against the publishing house that had reneged on its promise to publish her book. Now she planned to follow up her letter bomb with further acts of sabotage and violence.

First of all, she disguised herself as an employee of a gas company, saying she had come to check out a possible leak in the publishers' basement. Engineering an opportunity to be left on her own, she first made some dangerous adjustments to the freight lift and then started a small blaze in one corner of the book archive. By the time it had really taken hold and been discovered, she was out of the building and away. The fire causcd a great deal of damage and nearly claimed the life of a senior member of staff.

Later, an unsuspecting employee was seriously injured in a lift accident. The next day, a director of the company was fishcd out of a river, drowned. Suicide, everyone presumed – though, of course, the author and the reader knew better...

There was just an instant, when she read the part about the fire in the basement, that Calico felt a frisson of alarm. It was so uncannily similar to what had happened that morning. And added to the letter-bomb incident the day before...

But as she read on and the action became ever more wild and improbable, Calico relaxed, her opinion of Nemesis as a self-important, pathetic attention-seeker reaffirmed.

She tossed the manuscript aside for return with another standard rejection note and concentrated on reading some of the others in the pile. It was a desperate task. She could not have believed how bad the submissions could be. How could these people possibly think that such trash was worthy of publication? After ploughing through half a dozen awful sample chapters, she had just about had enough. She was not at all sorry, therefore, when the door to Elizabeth McIntyre's office opened and Austen Porter stepped out. Looking up, Calico met his gaze and was taken aback by its fury. The meeting had been remarkably quiet, but evidently it had not been amicable.

"She's gone too far," Austen Porter said, as much to himself as to Calico, and in a tone of undisguised loathing. "This time she's gone too far and she'll pay for it."

He turned to walk away, then stopped, turned back as if he'd forgotten something. "Don't be taken in by her, Calico," he said, the habitual sneer back on his face. "Don't be taken in by that vicious gorgon." Then he turned once more and strode away.

9

If Austen Porter was angry, Elizabeth McIntyre was ecstatic. She emerged from her office at half-past five that afternoon looking like a cat who'd just had a double helping of cream, and sent Calico down to the kitchen to fetch up a bottle of champagne.

"I feel like a celebration!" she said, cheerily.

When Calico came back with the required bottle, April Street was in Ms McIntyre's office. April, who had been speaking as Calico appeared, immediately clammed up.

"It's OK, April, Calico's on our side. Aren't you, Calico?" Elizabeth McIntyre exhorted.

"Well, yes," said Calico. Then, realizing this must sound less than convincing, explained, "I mean I don't really know what's going on."

"Well, sit down and you shall find out," Elizabeth

McIntyre said. "April, crack open that bottle," she commanded. "Let's have a drink."

But April didn't move. "I'm afraid I can't stay, Elizabeth," she said, coolly. "I've got an appointment."

"Well, you can stay for one drink, surely?"

"No, Elizabeth, I can't," April insisted. "I have to go now. You have one for me."

"Oh, all right," said Elizabeth McIntyre, with the gracelessness of one who was used to getting her own way.

"I don't know what's got in to April lately," Elizabeth McIntyre remarked when she judged April Street to be safely out of hearing. "She seems so – I don't know, distant, cold. What do you think of her?"

The question rather caught Calico on the hop.

"Well, she seems quite preoccupied," she offered tentatively. "But then things have been, well, preoccupying, haven't they?"

Elizabeth McIntyre laughed. "Yes," she agreed, "you could say that. And it's only just beginning…" She popped the cork on the bottle and poured champagne into two glasses.

"Here's to Prairie Books," she said, raising her glass flamboyantly, "and to its continued independence." She chinked her glass against Calico's and then drank deeply.

Calico took a small sip of her champagne and put the glass down on the table in front of her. Elizabeth McIntyre observed her keenly.

"You don't really drink, do you?"

"No," said Calico.

"And you don't smoke, either." She shook her head in amazement. "I thought you youngsters were supposed to be wild and uninhibited and indulgent." She gave Calico a sharp smile. "I guess I've read too many books," she conceded. Then she went on, "Was that a copy of *The Embryo Clinic* I saw on your desk?"

Calico nodded. "I'm halfway through," she said. "I'm really enjoying it."

Elizabeth McIntyre smiled again, with real warmth this time.

"I'm glad," she said simply. She paused a moment, then added, "I suppose you'd like to know what it is we're celebrating?"

"Well, yes," Calico confessed wryly. At last, it seemed, all was to be revealed.

Elizabeth McIntyre embellished the story she had been telling a couple of evenings before. When Dale Jefferson Senior had been diagnosed as having cancer, she said, he had been determined that the publishing house he had established would not die with him. He had already baulked a number of take-over bids from various multinational publishing conglomerates and now he made arrangements to ensure that after his death Prairie Books would remain independent.

So he set up a trust, giving away fifty-one per cent of the company to a trust composed of the employees of the company and selected authors. The remaining forty-nine per cent of the shares were owned by his son, Dale Jefferson Junior. Now Elizabeth McIntyre had learned what she had long suspected: Dale Junior wanted to sell. He had been made an offer that he felt he could not – did not want to – refuse, an offer that would make him, personally, a massive fortune.

Elizabeth McIntyre had discovered this through a friend who worked for the conglomerate involved and had presumed that she would know about it. After all, she was one of the three trustees empowered by Dale Jefferson Senior to administer the trust – the others being Dale Junior himself and Judy Price.

Now, said Elizabeth McIntyre, everything made sense. Dale's decision to go up-market and offload such contentious authors as Marvin Adams was not for the good of the company, but to make it appear more attractive to a literary predator. It was all being done for his own personal gain and glory.

Calico was puzzled. "But I don't understand," she said, frowning. "Why are we celebrating? This all sounds awful."

"Ah," the editor intoned after refilling her glass for the fourth time, "the point is that Dale won't get away with it. He and Austen can manoeuvre all they like, but it will do them no good. I went to see the company lawyer this morning – that's why I was late. To sell, at least two of the trustees must be in favour and they're not. Dale knows I won't go along with his plan – this company loses its independence over my dead body – but he thinks he can persuade Judy. Well, he can't. Oh, she may not see eye to eye with me on everything but on this issue we think as one: no sale. And there's no way she's going to change her mind, no way. So Dale and Austen can go hang." Elizabeth McIntyre drained her glass and smiled victoriously.

Watching her, Calico recalled the furious expression on Austen Porter's face earlier. The memory prompted a question.

"But what does Austen stand to gain from a take-over?" she asked.

Elizabeth McIntyre acknowledged the question with a knowing nod. "Ah, yes, that's something else I learned from my friend," she said. "If the deal goes through, Prairie Books becomes a literary imprint and Austen gets to be publisher."

"And what about you?" Calico fired the question without thinking.

In response, Elizabeth McIntyre made an inelegant gesture with her thumb. "I get the push," she said.

The effort to absorb all this information and its implications had set Calico's mind spinning as surely as if she had drunk all the champagne she'd been offered. Then it came to her suddenly that she had made a tentative arrangement with Romy to go to the cinema that night and that her aunt would be expecting to hear from her. It struck her also that this gave her the perfect excuse to get away – she'd had enough of Prairie Books for the week.

"Oh, right, yes, of course," spluttered Elizabeth McIntyre when Calico made her excuse. "I shouldn't have kept you so long. I was thinking April would be here…" She looked a little mournful for a second or two, before returning to her businesslike self. "Could you run a couple of errands for me before you go?"

"Of course," said Calico.

Elizabeth McIntyre gave her a note to drop into Judy Price's tray. Judy had not been in the office today and still no one seemed to know where she was, though the general opinion seemed to be that she had gone off to her country retreat, as she did from time to time. She never stayed more than a couple of days, but as there was no phone there, she was quite uncontactable. Elizabeth wanted to be sure that her fellow trustee had all the facts about Dale's intentions in front of her the instant she returned.

"Then, perhaps you could take one of these boxes to the lift for me," the editor asked, indicating two small but well-stocked cardboard boxes. "I always take a pile of manuscripts home on a Friday night," she explained. "It keeps me going over the weekend."

"Oh," Calico said, admiring her boss's diligence while at the same time thinking it was something she'd never want to do. The weekend was for having fun.

The production department was over the other

side of the building. To get to it Calico had to walk through a number of other departments, all of them deserted at this hour. It gave her an eerie feeling, walking by all those peopleless desks, many of which were still cluttered with the work of the day. But the building was not as utterly deserted as she had presumed. As she approached Austen Porter's office, she heard voices. One of them belonged to the sneering editor himself, but it was the other that made Calico stop where she stood. Austen Porter was talking with April Street.

"She has to go," said Austen sharply. "And if she won't go voluntarily, which she won't, of course, then she has to be got rid of."

"Kill her off, you mean," said April, with an icy amusement that sent a shiver down Calico's spine. "Yes, I like that. And why not kill the other off while you're at it?"

"Jude?" Austen queried. He sniggered unpleasantly. "Well, it's a nice thought, but I'm not sure we'd get away with that, are you?"

"Perhaps not," April agreed. Then she laughed too, but with malice rather than pleasure. Calico shivered again.

"Well," said April. "I think it's time I went."

There was the sound of a chair scraping the floor and suddenly Calico realized in a panic that at any moment April would appear out in the corridor and see her standing there. Quickly and quietly, she opened the door of the office next to Austen's and squeezed in. She stood in the dark, pressed against the wall, hardly daring to breathe, until at last she heard Austen and April walk by and away down the corridor. Then she breathed out heavily.

As she walked the rest of the way to production and then back again, Calico tried to make sense of what she'd just overheard. It sounded like a plot against Elizabeth McIntyre and if it was, then it meant that April Street had turned on her long-time associate. Whatever, she certainly seemed to be thick as thieves with Austen Porter and he was definitely the enemy as far as Elizabeth McIntyre was concerned. So what was going on? "Kill her off," they'd said and Calico didn't like the sound of that at all. The suggestion had been made with such a callous tone. She'd have to tell Elizabeth McIntyre, and warn her.

Elizabeth McIntyre was on the phone when Calico got back to her office, so she picked up one of the cardboard boxes and carried it along the corridor to the lift. As she arrived, she bumped into Austen Porter, coming away from the area of the lift. He looked startled for an instant, but his eyes quickly regained their poise. He glared at her with open hostility. "Oh, it's you," he sneered, his thin face the epitome of contempt. Then he walked away towards his office.

"I know what you're up to," muttered Calico under her breath. Then she summoned the lift. She'd had quite enough of office politics. *Roll on the weekend*, she thought.

When the lift appeared she pulled back the heavy, concertina outer door and the cage gate within, and pushed the box inside. The lift was a very basic-looking contraption – bare beaten-metal floor and tinny, cream walls – designed to carry freight, not people. Prairie Books was only on four levels, anyway, so it was much quicker to use the stairs. It was for Fred's use really and he didn't take kindly to anyone else riding in it. Not that Calico, for one, was remotely tempted.

She met Elizabeth McIntyre just leaving her office, carrying the second box.

"I've called a cab," said the editor. "Can I drop you somewhere?"

Calico nodded. "Thank you," she said. "I just have to call my aunt quickly first. Is that OK?"

"Of course," said Ms McIntyre, with the flushed *bonhomie* of one who had just consumed the best part of a bottle of champagne. "I'll meet you in reception."

The cab journey, thought Calico, would give her the perfect opportunity to bring Elizabeth McIntyre up to date with what she'd just heard.

Romy thought it best if they postpone their visit to the cinema until the following evening.

"You've had a hard week, dear," she said, "and it sounds like you've got a lot to tell me about. Get back, have a long soak in the bath and I'll order us a takeaway."

Calico readily agreed. By the time she got home it would be eight-thirty and even now she felt herself flagging. She said goodbye and put down the receiver. As she did so, something caught her eye in the address book that lay open on Elizabeth McIntyre's desk. It was an address. A box number. PO Box 111. *The address she was looking at was the address that appeared at the top of each of the Nemesis letters...*

Barely had she registered this fact, however, than the quiet around her was broken by a terrible scream.

10

The lift had fallen. The door to the shaft wouldn't open, but peering through the small window in it, Calico could see to her horror that one of the steel lift cables had snapped. The lift was wedged against the wall of the shaft, midway between floors.

"Ms McIntyre!" she cried. "Ms McIntyre! Are you all right?"

The response was a muffled moan. Evidently the editor was not in great shape. As if in sympathy, the surviving lift cable groaned too, suggesting the weight it was holding was too much to bear... Calico's heart raced. She could feel the veins throbbing in her head as she agonized over what to do. She should get help. But what if the lift gave way while she was gone? No, she had to try.

"Hold on, Ms McIntyre!" she called. "I'm going

to get help." She flew along the corridor down to Austen Porter's office. But the lights were out now, the room empty. She was alone in the building. The realization caused a flush of heat to rise through her body and for a moment she was paralysed by panic. Then she reached for the nearest phone and dialled the emergency services...

By the time she got back to the lift, the cable's groaning had grown more pronounced and insistent. She called out to her boss again, but this time received no reply. She had to get into the lift, but how, when the door was shut tight? Standing back, she suddenly saw the answer. On the wall above the lift-button was a small hole and, above that, held in a bracket, was a metal rod.

She reached up and took down the rod. Then she pushed it into the hole and turned. There was a click. Now when Calico tried the lift door, it opened easily. She peered into the gloom. At first all she could make out was the dirty brickwork of the shaft walls and the thick metal poles that stood against them; below, the top of the sloping lift was just a blur of dark metal.

Gradually, her eyes grew more accustomed to the gloom and she could see the remaining lift cable. What she saw worried her greatly. The cable was made up of three steel strands, each of which appeared to be badly frayed. It didn't look as if the cable would hold for very long. Peering down again, she thought she glimpsed an arm, protruding from inside the lift. It was very still and very limp… She needed to do something – and quickly.

Grabbing the rod-key, she sped away once more along the corridor, this time making for the stairs. She climbed down one flight and then ran to the lift point, where she repeated the process she'd carried out on the floor above with the rod and the hole in the wall. As before, the door lock released. The door itself was stiff and difficult to open, but, adrenalin pumping, Calico forced it back.

Here the situation was more clearly visible: the lift really was hanging at an alarming angle. Standing just inside the door and craning her head, Calico could see Elizabeth McIntyre through a gap between the side of the lift and the shaft wall, slumped on the floor by the inner cage door. There was blood on her forehead.

"Ms McIntyre!" she called again, in desperation.

"Calico?" came the feeble, questioning reply. But at least it was a reply.

"I've called the emergency services," Calico said. "You're going to be rescued." But no sooner had she spoken than the lift gave a weary lurch and dropped a little more, opening the gap between the lift and the shaft wall; one of the strands, evidently, had given up the ghost – which meant only two remained intact. Elizabeth McIntyre cried out in shock and pain.

The shift in the lift's position revealed the injured woman more fully. Indeed, if she were to reach up, Calico could almost touch her.

"Are you badly hurt?" she enquired.

"I hit my head," Elizabeth McIntyre responded weakly. "And my ankle aches horribly."

"Do you think you can move?" Calico asked, pleaded almost.

"I could try," said the editor. There was a sudden anguished yelp as she did just that. "I'm not sure I can," she said. The lift twitched again.

"I think you're going to have to," Calico said grimly. "The lift's not going to hold much longer. You've got to get out of there." Then she made a decision. "I'm coming to help you."

"No, it's too dangerous," said Elizabeth McIntyre, squeezing some of her customary imperiousness through the sharp pain she was obviously feeling. But to no avail. Calico was already inching her way out, levering herself up on the sturdy steel poles that ran parallel to the shaft walls, and searching for footholds. In a matter of moments, she was opposite the lift's cage door. Reaching out, she found the handle and wrenched the door back.

"Take my hand," she said, extending a hand towards the prone figure in front of her.

"Calico, you shouldn't..." Elizabeth McIntyre began, but her words tailed off into an exclamation of pain as she stretched to take hold of the proffered hand.

"Grip hard," Calico pleaded. "Pull yourself towards me."

It was a slow, tortuous process. Elizabeth

McIntyre's face was deathly pale and she was perspiring heavily. Mascara smudged her cheekbones. But, eventually, she got herself to the edge of the lift. As she did so, though, the lift lurched once more as another strand in the lift cable gave way.

Calico had to react quickly, pushing out her hand to stop Elizabeth McIntyre tumbling from the heavily tilting lift and down into the shaft. For an instant or so the two women stayed silent, breathing deeply, trying to recover their equilibrium.

"Now you've just got to climb out here next to me," said Calico at last.

"Oh, is that all?" the editor replied haltingly, with a pinched smile.

Calico helped her boss find a handhold without too much difficulty, but getting the rest of her to follow was no easy task. In the end, Calico put one foot in the lift to give the older woman some support. She did it gingerly, afraid that exerting too much pressure might be the straw that broke the camel's back and the cable would finally snap altogether. It was at this moment that Calico first really registered the peril she was in. A new outbreak of metallic groaning from above intensified her alarm.

"I don't think I can do this, Calico," Elizabeth McIntyre gasped helplessly. She looked as if she were about to collapse from exhaustion. But Calico was in no mood to allow her boss to give in now.

"You're nearly there. Just one more push," she urged, almost prising the editor's back leg from the lift floor. With a last heroic effort, Elizabeth McIntyre managed to drag her injured leg across the gap and find a resting place on the wall.

"You did it!" Calico shouted. But her triumphant cry was silenced almost at once, as the last strand in the lift cable finally succumbed. Feeling the floor shift beneath her, Calico flung herself out and flat against the wall. She flinched and yelled as the top edge of the lift crunched in to the brickwork close by her head then bounced out again and dropped away down the shaft, smashing violently against the walls as it fell, until, eventually, it came to a crashing halt at the bottom.

Calico bit her lip, but she couldn't stop the tears welling beneath her tightly-shut lids. She swallowed hard, inhaled shakily, her body racked now by silent sobs. In the sudden tranquil stillness, she felt a hand wrap itself around her own.

"It's OK, Calico," Elizabeth McIntyre breathed. "You did brilliantly."

But Calico wasn't reassured. Relieved as she was that her rescue attempt had succeeded, she knew that things weren't OK. Not by a long way.

In her head one word went round and round, pervasive as the dust that whirled now in the void of the shaft, disturbed by the lift's fall: *Nemesis*.

11

Calico was exhausted. She slept most of Saturday and, when she did finally wake, Romy insisted she stay in bed and rest. Which was fine by Calico. Her only worry was that Elizabeth McIntyre was OK, but Romy soon reassured her on this point – the redoubtable editor was to remain in hospital for a second night, but mainly for observation. Her injuries, happily, had been relatively minor: a gashed head and slight concussion, heavy bruising to the arms and ribs and a twisted ankle. When Romy had phoned the hospital at lunchtime, she had been informed that Elizabeth McIntyre was recovering well from her ordeal and might be discharged later the following day.

"We could go and see her in the morning, if you like," Romy suggested to her niece. "If you feel up to it."

"Yes, I'd like to," Calico said emphatically. "I'm fine, really. Just tired." She wanted to see Elizabeth McIntyre. There were things she had to tell her. Right now, though, she needed some time to think.

When Romy went downstairs to prepare some food, Calico lay back and ran through the events of the night before. She hoped this might clarify matters, but all it seemed to do was muddy the waters, throwing up a plethora of seemingly unanswerable questions...

She thought about April in Austen's office and the conversation she'd overheard. Was it Elizabeth McIntyre they were talking about? Surely it had to be. "*If she won't go voluntarily, then she has to be got rid of,*" they'd said and April had laughed. Calico recalled running into Austen Porter by the lift just before the accident and the startled, almost guilty look on his face, as if she'd caught him doing something he shouldn't have been doing. Like sabotaging the lift? No, it was incredible. Sure, he wanted Elizabeth McIntyre out of the way, but *murder*? That was the sort of thing that only happened in books, wasn't it? Besides, there was a far more glaring culprit. At the centre of all the murkiness, one name gleamed with malice beyond question: *Nemesis*.

When the police had interviewed Calico at the hospital, she'd told them about Nemesis. She'd related pretty much word for word the contents of the two letters and the main incidents contained in the manuscripts: the letter bomb, the lift accident, the death of a director. The first two events had been precisely forecast and the third had nearly come true as well: nobody was in any doubt that Elizabeth McIntyre would have plunged to her death in the falling lift if Calico had not come to her aid.

Foul play was certainly suspected as the cause of the accident, but the police were still of the opinion that the pro-life terrorists were to blame. They'd never come across this "Nemesis" before, they said, but it could well be an extremist splinter group or possibly a single hard-line member of the terrorist organization acting alone.

They took details of the Nemesis box number and the name Calico had seen alongside it in Elizabeth McIntyre's address book. They'd really wanted to talk to Elizabeth McIntyre herself, but she'd been in no state to be interviewed. Fatigued from pain and her exertions, she'd collapsed in the ambulance and, soon after arrival at the hospital, had fallen into a deep sleep. The doctors would not allow her to be disturbed.

Calico considered again the name she had read in Ms McIntyre's book: Rose Marie Church. It was a name that seemed somehow familiar. Was it an author, perhaps? That would explain, certainly, why it was in the editor's address book, though not why it had two diagonal lines through it, seemingly crossing it out. She needed to know more... When Romy returned some minutes later with a tray, bearing a large Spanish omelette, an appetizing salad and a

75

tumbler of sparkling mineral water, Calico quizzed her about Rose Marie Church. At the mention of the name, Romy's expression grew immediately sad.

"At one time," she said, "we were quite close."

"Is she an author?" Calico asked.

Romy nodded. "She was. A very good one," she said. "Very successful, too. Her books were enormously popular."

"Does she still write?" Calico persisted.

Romy shook her head. "As far as I know, she hasn't published a book for ten years."

"What happened to her?" asked Calico.

"I don't really know," said Romy, with a thoughtful look. "She simply disappeared." She looked meaningfully at the food in front of her niece, which Calico took as a silent prompt to start eating.

"Could you tell me about her?" she asked, cutting a morsel of omelette and raising it to her mouth.

As Calico ate her food – soon realizing just how hungry she was – Romy told her a little about Rose Marie Church. She had written mystery stories, ingenious whodunnits with a touch of the macabre, set around the turn of the sixteenth century. She'd been dubbed the new "Queen of Crime", or as one reviewer had it, "Agatha Christie in doublet and hose". When Romy's first book had been published Rose Marie Church had been at the height of her fame. She was one of the most read authors of the day. Romy had met her at an award ceremony at which the celebrated author had been presented with a special prize for her outstanding contribution to the crime novel genre. Rose Marie Church, Romy recalled, had made an extraordinary impression: dressed all in black, from black hat and veil to black heels, she had even worn black lipstick.

"She was amazingly striking, a publicist's dream," Romy said. "That was the first time she'd been seen in public for several years. She was a very private person, you see – a recluse, really. I met her in the loos. She was hiding out there, sitting in one of the cubicles, smoking, when I went in to have a pee. It was towards the end of the evening, I remember, and I was about to go home, but instead I ended up listening to Rose Marie pouring out her woes. And she had some woes, poor woman."

"Did you become friends?" Calico asked.

Her aunt blew out her lips in a questioning pout. "Friends?" she said. "Well, I suppose you could say so. That award ceremony was the last public event Rose Marie attended. She withdrew completely after that. Even those of us she liked rarely saw her. My friendship with Rose Marie was almost entirely conducted through correspondence. We wrote to each other often. She was a great letter writer."

"I can see why you got on," Calico said, with sly affection. "But what happened to her? Why did she stop writing?"

"I don't honestly know," Romy confessed.

She went on to tell Calico that Rose Marie Church had been published by Prairie Books, but the association had been discontinued soon after Elizabeth McIntyre started at the company. She didn't know why exactly, but the rumour was that the editor had turned down a new novel or asked for major changes which Rose Marie Church had refused to make. The novel never appeared and, in time, sales of the author's titles fell away. Rose Marie Church herself disappeared.

"I think she had some kind of breakdown," Romy said. "The last letters she sent me were very dark, wild – very bitter. Abusive, even. I felt that my letters were just fuelling her anger, so I stopped writing back. Then I went to Rome for six months with my first husband, Richard, and when I came back she had gone, vanished. I haven't heard from her since, nor has anyone else as far as I know."

Romy paused reflectively. "She was a great friend of Marvin Adams at that time," she added. "He was one of the very few people she actually saw."

Calico had just put down her fork and was about to ask another question when her aunt pre-empted her.

"Why all this interest in Rose Marie?" she asked.

Briefly, Calico told Romy about the Nemesis letters and manuscripts and about Rose Marie Church's address being the same as the Nemesis box number.

"Yes, I always corresponded with Rose Marie at a box number," Romy said. "I never knew her actual address. She had a mania for privacy, even with those she knew well." She looked hard at Calico for an instant and pursed her lips grimly. "Rose Marie was quite a disturbed person and she had a dark, brilliant imagination. It wouldn't surprise me that she would use the name Nemesis, but why write to Elizabeth, now, after all this time? And, as for trying to kill her... No, that I can't believe. With Rose Marie, it was all in the mind, she lived in her imagination. I don't believe she'd be capable of such action."

"But how else can you explain the things in the manuscripts?" Calico queried. "You don't think that's coincidence, surely."

"It would be a very extraordinary one," her aunt agreed. "I just can't believe Rose Marie could be responsible for such outrages. Not the Rose Marie I knew, strange as she was."

"But you did say you haven't heard from her for ten years," Calico pointed out. "Who knows what might have happened to her in that time? Perhaps she *did* have a major breakdown. She might be completely different now, stranger, much more bitter..."

Romy sighed. "I suppose you're right," she said. "I just hope it isn't so." Her emerald eyes looked so unhappy that Calico felt a little guilty.

"I'd love to see her books, if you have any of them," she said, introducing a lighter note. "It'll give me something to do while I'm resting."

"Yes, of course," Romy agreed. "I've got one somewhere. A signed copy. I'll get it for you."

The book she brought back was called *Men Beware*

Women. The title, Romy said, was taken from a Jacobean tragedy, *Women Beware Women*, by Thomas Middleton. The front cover showed a dead man slumped over a desk with a quill pen dripping blood.

On the back cover there was a large black and white photograph of the author. It was true: Rose Marie Church was very striking. Her eyes, in particular, were very arresting. Dark, intense, almost desperate, they stared out at Calico as if in a plea for understanding. "Please, like me," they seemed to say. It took Calico rather by surprise. She'd expected someone older, fiercer, sinister-looking; she hadn't expected to find Rose Marie Church so appealing.

This impression was confirmed when she turned to the title page and read its brief, handwritten message: "*To dear Romy, fellow scribbler and felicitous friend*" – under which the author had signed her full name. Reading this, Calico comprehended her aunt's inability to believe that Rose Marie Church could be responsible for the outrages at Prairie Books over the past few days; she found it pretty difficult to credit herself. Until she turned the page. Then all her earlier damning suspicions returned with a vengeance. For opposite the first page of the story was a quotation, and its final words were all too familiar.

" 'Who can perceive this?' " Calico read. " 'Save that eternal eye that sees through flesh and all?' "

The words did not appear exactly as in Nemesis's second letter, but they were close enough for Calico to be sure that they were drawn from the same source. She gazed at the title, printed beneath the quotation: *The Revenger's Tragedy*, it said. Calico frowned. Rose Marie Church, it seemed, was after revenge. But why exactly – and against who? Well, whatever the answers, one thing was plain: she'd stop at nothing to get it…

12

12

runner. She could more or less picture her anyway. Very attractive. They were all very attractive. Calico stood up from her chair and felt, a moment way, very foreign as she usually stood against a wall. With whatever little room conditions may prevail at an exciting event.

Arriving at the hospital next morning, Calico and Romy found Elizabeth McIntyre sitting up in bed, looking amazingly well-groomed and composed. Her hair was neat and brushed-out and she was wearing make-up; the bandage around her forehead was the only evidence of the ordeal she'd been through. Not for the first time, Calico was filled with admiration as she considered her boss. She seemed so, well, indestructible, a phenomenon. She felt a sudden surge of pride at the thought that she was assistant to this remarkable woman.

"Romy, how lovely to see you!" Elizabeth McIntyre uttered with genuine pleasure. "And Calico. How are you, you star?"

"I'm fine," Calico said, smiling shyly.

"Good," said Elizabeth McIntyre. Then she

turned to Romy. "She saved my life, you know, Romy." Both women looked at Calico, who blushed under their gaze.

"I just did what I had to," she said, modestly.

"You did brilliantly," Elizabeth McIntyre insisted.

They talked for a while about the incident on Friday night. Elizabeth McIntyre said she'd felt sure she was going to die. She'd never even have tried to escape from the lift if Calico hadn't been there to cajole and assist her. She hadn't thought at the time that someone was trying to kill her, and even when the police had told her earlier that morning that the lift had definitely been sabotaged, she'd found it hard to believe. She knew she wasn't exactly the most popular person at Prairie Books at present, but it seemed incredible that someone hated her so much as to try to murder her.

It was then that Calico told her boss about the Nemesis letters and manuscripts.

"I was going to tell you about the letters before," she said. "But April said not to bother. She thought they were just some kind of joke. So did I – until last night." She grimaced, but Elizabeth McIntyre was quite unmoved. She nodded knowingly. Then without speaking, she reached for her bag and, after a brief rummage, produced a letter in a black envelope. She handed it to Calico.

"Read it," she exhorted. "It was sent to me at home a couple of days ago."

Calico glanced briefly at the envelope then, heart

pounding, she slid out the letter inside.

"Oh!" she exclaimed as she recognized the box number at the head of the page. Her gaze fell quickly to the signature. "*Nemesis*," she breathed.

The style was different from the other letters but the message was just as menacing. This time, though, there was no mystery or ambiguity, no talk of "the eternal eye" or anything weird like that. This was a straightforward attack, personal and abusive. Elizabeth McIntyre was "a selfish bitch sacrificing others' happiness on the altar of her ambition"; she was "a woman of no principles", "disloyal and dismissive of the efforts of others" and, the letter promised, she would get her comeuppance very soon. All of which was a far cry from the veiled threats of the previous letters. Romy had alluded to the author's dark side, and now it appeared that dark side had taken over entirely. And there was no doubt any more, Calico realized, who was the target of the author's hatred. It was Elizabeth McIntyre.

"I can't think who would send me such a letter," the editor remarked, as Calico passed the Nemesis missive to her aunt.

"I can," Calico said simply. Then she told Elizabeth McIntyre about her discovery the evening before.

"Rose Marie Church!" Elizabeth McIntyre said incredulously. "But that's absurd. I haven't had any contact with her for ages, *years*. I hardly knew her."

"Some people harbour grudges for ever," Romy said, grimly.

Elizabeth McIntyre shook her bandaged head dismissively. "I still can't believe it," she said. "I mean, why start *now*? If she wanted to harm me, surely she'd have done it years ago, when I rejected her last book."

"It does seem strange, I admit," Romy agreed. The two women lapsed into a thoughtful silence.

Calico watched them for a moment, then she said a little tentatively, "Why *did* you reject Rose Marie Church's book?"

Elizabeth McIntyre looked at her assistant quizzically. "I read one of her books yesterday," Calico continued, "and I thought it was really good, really gripping, you know. It seemed, well, like your sort of book."

Elizabeth McIntyre nodded. "Very astute, Calico," she said. "I did like Rose Marie Church's books a lot. I thought she was an excellent writer, until I came to edit her. Her manuscript was one of the first I received when I started at Prairie Books." She gave a wry grin. "I guess you could call it a baptism of fire."

The problem was, Elizabeth McIntyre explained, that Rose Marie Church's manuscript was not like her other books – the books that had made her such a popular favourite. It wasn't a mystery story at all. It was a very heavy, gloomy tale about relationships, written in a rather self-conscious, flowery style. She wanted to be regarded as a serious, literary writer, she'd said. But the book was dull, wooden, and quite unpublishable according to Elizabeth McIntyre. No one would read it, she thought, and it would disappoint Rose Marie Church's many fans.

She wasn't the only one who thought so, either. Judy Price had read the manuscript, too, and she'd been even more damning. Elizabeth McIntyre had written a detailed letter to the author with her criticisms and had tried to persuade her to return to her former style, to write another Jacobean thriller. But Rose Marie Church wouldn't. Her curt reply insisted that Elizabeth McIntyre publish the manuscript that had been delivered. Elizabeth McIntyre refused. A few days later, she received a letter from Nina Mallinson stating that Rose Marie Church no longer wished to be published by Prairie Books, and she had heard nothing of the author since.

It was a strange, rather pathetic story. As she listened, Calico felt some sympathy for Rose Marie Church, but she felt more for Elizabeth McIntyre. It couldn't be easy being an editor, she thought. You had to be strong and make tough decisions. You had to do what you thought was right even if it meant upsetting people. It wasn't fair that Elizabeth McIntyre should be persecuted like this. She had only been doing her job and she deserved respect. Well, she had Calico's, that was for sure.

"What happened to the book you rejected," she asked now. "Did it ever get published?"

Elizabeth McIntyre shook her head. "No, I don't believe so," she said. She wrinkled her nose. "It really wasn't very good."

"What was it called?" Calico enquired, intrigued. "Do you remember?"

Elizabeth McIntyre pondered this question for an instant or two. Then her face opened out as if she'd just made a shocking discovery.

"Yes," she said. "I do remember. The book was called *Nemesis*."

13

There was no doubt about it, Elizabeth McIntyre was an exceptional woman. Calico could hardly believe it when she came in to Prairie Books on Monday morning to discover her boss already installed and hard at work. She'd tied a red silk scarf around her head to cover up her bandage, so there was no visible sign of her injury. As ever, she looked the picture of style and elegance.

"Ms McIntyre," Calico said in amazement, standing in the doorway to the editor's office. "Shouldn't you still be in bed?"

Elizabeth McIntyre waved her hand dismissively. "I've got far too much to do," she said. "And anyway, I'm really quite all right now." She touched the scarf on her head. "A little scratch on the head's not going to keep me away." She looked at Calico shrewdly.

"The way things are, I might never be allowed back."

Calico went along the corridor to get Ms McIntyre some coffee. She was standing by the machine when the chairman marched up, clutching a newspaper in one hand.

"Is Elizabeth in?" he demanded curtly, his voice cool yet devoid of its usual suavity. Indeed, his whole appearance was untypically ruffled. His fair hair looked like it needed brushing, his complexion was a little florid, his bow tie slightly askew. It was obvious at a glance that he was in a state of strong emotion.

"Yes, she is," Calico answered.

"Right," said the chairman and his voice was hard with fury.

The confrontation that followed was the fiercest Calico had experienced since starting at Prairie Books. It was also very one-sided. The door to the editor's office remained open throughout, so Calico could hear every word – most of them spoken by Dale Jefferson. Given the injuries and the ordeal Elizabeth McIntyre had so recently suffered, Calico expected the chairman might show her some sympathy. But not a bit of it. From the instant Dale Jefferson Junior entered the room, he launched a tirade of insult and accusation at the editorial director. He accused her of leaking news of the pro-posed "merger" to the press. He called it an action of inexcusable selfishness and spite. She was trying to hold the company back, he said, by deliberately attempting to ruin a deal that was of benefit to everyone. He called her a "vicious, self-centred harridan" and said that she was acting like a character from one of her own tawdry books.

What shocked Calico most of all, though, was his suggestion that Elizabeth McIntyre was in some way to blame for the accidents that had occurred during the previous week. She'd do anything to make the company look like a bad investment, he said. But it wouldn't work. The merger would go ahead with or without her. There was nothing she could do to stop it. His final words held an ominous threat. "Be clear on this, Elizabeth," he warned with cold malignity. "Anyone who tries to stand against this venture will be swept away, *destroyed*. I shall see to it personally."

As he stormed away, Dale Jefferson threw the newspaper he'd been holding on to the floor by Calico's desk. Intrigued, she picked it up to see what it was that had got the chairman into such a fury. Her eyes alighted on a bold headline halfway down the page. "Publisher Sells Out", it read. The article underneath began by reporting the projected deal to sell Prairie Books to a much bigger publisher, the details of which were pretty much as Elizabeth McIntyre had told Calico a few days before.

Then there was a brief résumé of the history of the company, praising the populist vision of Dale Jefferson Senior and attacking the literary pretensions of his son, who was portrayed as a vain glory-seeker, looking down his nose at the kind of thumping good read that had made Prairie Books so successful. A cartoon alongside the article portrayed Dale Jefferson Junior as a fat peacock, standing proudly, while all his feathers fell off. No wonder he was so angry!

The knives were really out for Elizabeth McIntyre now, thought Calico, as she put the paper in the bin. With April Street's allegiance extremely doubtful and Judy Price still absent, it seemed as though she, Calico, was the editor's only sure ally. Well, she would stand firm. What had happened on Friday night had brought them together in a special way. A bond had been formed between them and Calico was determined it should not be broken. She wouldn't buckle before the threats of the Chairman or Austen Porter or Nemesis or anyone else. She'd support Elizabeth McIntyre against them all.

"As if Elizabeth McIntyre could have been responsible for the fire, or that accident in the lift," Calico complained to Joy and Dan later down in the post-room. "He should have seen her face when I was trying to help her. She was really terrified. She believed she was going to die."

"Of course she didn't fake it," said Dan, with uncharacteristic irritation. His sea-green, blue (just what colour *were* they?) eyes held Calico in a piercing stare. He looked unusually serious. "I'm responsible," he said.

Calico was totally taken aback. "Er, you?" she uttered. "I don't understand."

Dan sighed. "That lunchtime I was on my own in reception; Joy and Fred were at lunch." He glanced at Joy and she nodded. "Then some guy came in, said he was here to look at the lift. Routine maintenance he called it. Well, I know the lift's serviced regularly and the guy looked right, you know. He had all the equipment and stuff. I never thought for a second he might be, like, an imposter."

"You mean, he wasn't genuine?"

Dan shook his head. "The police checked. Our lift's not due for a service for another fortnight. The guy who came in on Friday wasn't from the lift company at all."

"He must have been the saboteur," Joy said.

Lights were flashing wildly in Calico's head and once again it was the word Nemesis they illuminated. This is what had happened in the manuscript, wasn't it? The avenging author had disguised herself to get into the publishing house.

"Did you get a good look at the person?" she asked Dan.

"Not very," Dan admitted, rather forlornly. "I didn't really pay much attention to the guy, to be honest. You know how many people come in and out of this place." His eyes appealed for her sympathy. "I gave the police the best description I could."

"You're sure it was a guy?" Calico queried. "It couldn't have been a woman in disguise?"

"A woman?" Dan repeated, intrigued. "You think it was a woman?"

"Why do you think it was a woman, Calico?" asked Joy.

Over the next few minutes, Calico brought Dan and Joy up to date with all that she had learned about Rose Marie Church. She told them her belief that the author was behind the attacks on Prairie Books and why. When she finished, Dan whistled.

"That's some story," he said, his easy geniality back in evidence now that he'd got his "confession" off his chest. "Worthy of a Jacobean tragedy, you know."

"Definitely," Calico agreed. "Which reminds me, Dan. The second Nemesis letter? The one you brought up the other day? It had this strange line in it about the 'eternal eye that sees all'. Well, I found out where it comes from: *The Revenger's Tragedy*. Rose Marie Church used the same quote in one of her books."

"*The Revenger's Tragedy*, eh?" Dan repeated with amused interest. "That's some play."

"Very bloody, too," Joy added dramatically, pulling an expression of distaste. "I played in it once, at college. Everybody dies."

"Yeah," Dan conceded. "It's bloody all right. But revenge is, isn't it?" He gave Calico a questioning look.

"Revenge is pointless if you ask me," she said emphatically. Dan's face settled into a freckly grin that made Calico smile too.

"*The Revenger's Tragedy* wouldn't be much of a play without it," he said.

At this point the conversation was brought to an

abrupt end by the appearance of Fred in the post-room. "Are you three going to stand there chattering all day?" he grumbled. "There's plenty of work to be done, you know." Then he shook his head glumly. "Editors," he tutted, with the air of a man who had been deeply wronged. Calico grinned at Dan. Obviously Fred held her responsible for disrupting his little kingdom.

"See you later," she said jauntily. Then with a wave to Joy, she beat a hasty retreat.

After the Chairman's early explosion, the day passed without further drama and Calico was able to concentrate on her work. There was plenty to do, too: calls to make and answer, letters to write, manuscripts to read, errands to run… At the end of the afternoon, she felt quite invigorated from her tasks, and ready for an evening out at the cinema with Romy. She thought, fleetingly, about asking Dan, but, well, maybe that was a bit pushy. She'd give it a bit longer.

Having made sure her desk was tidy, she got up to go, popping her head in at Elizabeth McIntyre's door on the way out to say goodbye. But as it happened she never said a word. She was struck totally silent by the sight of her boss, sitting motionless behind her desk, staring ahead, mouth open, face grey as a sunless sky.

"Ms McIntyre?" she murmured at last. "Are you all right? What is it?"

Slowly, as if in a dream, the editor turned her head towards Calico. Her face was like stone.

"They've found Jude," she said quietly. "Pulled her out of a river, drowned." Then as if this somehow wasn't clear enough, "Judy Price is dead," she added. And, hearing those words, Calico felt her veins turn to ice.

14

14

In the opinion of the police, there were no suspicious circumstances involved in Judy Price's death. She had either died as a result of a tragic accident or, more likely, she had committed suicide. Everyone knew that she had been under enormous strain. She'd had breakdowns in the past and her husband confirmed she had been depressed recently. Events at Prairie Books had really been getting to her... It was all plausible enough but then, thought Calico, that's exactly how Nemesis had planned it. She knew Judy Price hadn't taken her own life; Rose Marie Church had murdered her.

As if in proof of this, a third Nemesis letter arrived in the post the next afternoon. Calico's fingers trembled a little as she opened the envelope. As ever, it contained a brief letter and a couple of pages of manuscript. The familiar P O Box No. 111 headed the letter, which read, in block capitals,

DEAR MADAM,

HERE IS THE THIRD AND FINAL INSTALMENT OF MY STORY, PUBLISH OR DIE! I HOPE YOU READ AND DIGESTED THE PREVIOUS TWO. YOU WOULD DO WELL TO PAY PARTICULAR ATTENTION TO THIS INSTALMENT. IT WILL BE YOUR LAST. NOW IT IS TIME TO PAY...

AND YOU WILL PAY. MURDER'S QUIT-RENT MUST BE MET IN FULL.

NEMESIS

So this is it, thought Calico, grimly, as she put down the manuscript. There were to be no more "warnings". Nemesis was out to kill Elizabeth McIntyre. If that hadn't been obvious before, it was now. Calico even knew where and how the murder would happen. Ms McIntyre would be lured to the reference library on the floor above, where she would be drugged with chloroform and stabbed. It was all clearly set out in this latest and apparently last manuscript, which ended with the bitter author's murderous moment of revenge against the editor she felt had cheated her. Naturally, the criminal escaped undetected – her triumph complete.

As she sat at her desk, Calico's body hummed with purpose. The manuscript was a challenge, a gauntlet thrown down and she'd take it up. For certain no one else would. The police weren't interested in Rose Marie Church – they were still barking up their terrorist tree – and no one at Prairie Books was going to stick their necks out for someone viewed now as a company pariah. Dale Jefferson's memo to all staff the day before, extolling the virtues of the proposed "merger" and denouncing Elizabeth McIntyre's attempts to scupper it, had put the editor out on a limb. The sympathy that had been afforded her after the accidents of the previous week had now all but evaporated.

Picking up the Nemesis letter and manuscript, Calico went over to her boss's office.

"Another manuscript came," she said softly. "From Nemesis. I thought you'd want to see."

Elizabeth McIntyre took off her glasses and sighed. Judy Price's death, Calico observed, had hit her boss hard.

"What is it?" Elizabeth McIntyre enquired sharply. "More abuse? More puerile threats?" She shook her head. "No, I don't want to read it, Calico. Put it in the bin where it belongs." She rubbed her hand wearily over her forehead, touching the bandage that today she had made no attempt to hide. "I've had enough of this Nemesis business, Calico."

"But this time she's threatening to kill you," Calico persisted. "She even describes how she's going to do it. It's all here in the manuscript." This shocking revelation, however, had little effect on Elizabeth McIntyre.

"I really don't care, Calico," she said bitterly. "She can't hurt me now." There was an air of resignation in the editor's voice that Calico found disturbing.

"But she *can*," she insisted. "Everything she writes, well, it comes true. You should go away for a while."

Elizabeth McIntyre laughed a short mirthless laugh. "I'm not going anywhere," she said. "No one's going to make me leave. Anyway, where on earth would I go?"

Calico pondered this question as she sat back at her desk. Elizabeth McIntyre had no family, and few friends either, it seemed. Her work was her life, as she'd told Calico a couple of times already. There was one person, though, who Calico knew she liked and who liked her. She phoned Romy.

Calico's aunt was a little surprised at her niece's request to invite Elizabeth McIntyre to stay for a few days, but when the reason was explained she was perfectly willing.

"It would be nice to spend a little time with Elizabeth again," she said. "It's been a while since we had a good talk. I'll give her a call now if you like. We could have lunch and then take it from there."

"Thanks, Romy," said Calico. "You're the best."

"I *do* my best," Romy corrected her. "Now get off the phone and I'll ring Elizabeth…"

And so it was arranged. Calico wasn't at all sure that her boss would accept Romy's invitation, but she did, without demur. In fact, it actually seemed to lift her mood a little.

"Sometimes I forget how much I like Romy," she told Calico and there was a ghost of a smile on her pale lips. When Austen Porter appeared, demanding an "audience", she was back to her fighting best.

"It'll have to wait, Austen," she said, coolly. "I'm taking a couple of days off."

"Oh, fine," Austen remarked, his voice heavy with sarcasm. "Crucial decisions about the future of the company need to be taken and you're going on holiday. Terrific." His face took on a characteristic sneer. "But then you don't really care about the company's future, do you, Elizabeth?" But his goading failed to get a verbal response from Elizabeth McIntyre; she simply glared in silence at her fellow editor with a look of glowering disdain, until at last he turned and departed.

At lunch, having seen Elizabeth McIntyre leave in a cab to collect some things from her flat before going on to Romy's, Calico talked with Dan and Joy, filling them in on the latest developments.

"Elizabeth's much better off out of here," Joy remarked. "Especially after what happened to Judy Price."

"Working at Prairie Books is getting to be a very dangerous business," Dan added, grimly. "You'd better be careful, too, Calico. If Nemesis knows you're helping Elizabeth McIntyre, *you* may become a target." This suggestion sent a frisson of fear down

Calico's spine, but it was mixed with pleasure at Dan's evident concern for her welfare.

"I'll give Ms McIntyre all the help I can," she vowed. She looked from one to the other of her friends imploringly. "I could use some help, too, guys," she added.

"I'm with you," said Joy, giving Calico a flashing smile.

"Me, too," said Dan, his eyes recovering their sparkle, his face a warm spangle of freckles.

"Thanks," said Calico, appreciatively.

Dan and Joy were great allies to have, she thought; working in the reception area they could keep tabs on who came in and out and also what was going on. Joy, in particular, often received or overheard important snippets of information. People trusted and respected her – even the chairman had been known to confide in her. Her position and character put her at the hub of the company, while Dan's duties took him regularly to all parts of the building, delivering and collecting mail, shifting books and furniture...

"We should make quite a team," said Calico.

"The three musketeers," Joy suggested. And they all grinned, enjoying their adventure, united in their determination that Nemesis should not have it her own way...

Nemesis, however, was not to be taken lightly. Returning home that evening, Calico discovered the avenger had been in touch with Elizabeth McIntyre again. Another letter had arrived at her home, and like the previous one it was full of bitter denunciation and angry abuse: Elizabeth McIntyre was "a cheat", "a liar", a "two-faced user" and was promised "a bloody reckoning". It was as if Nemesis was drawing nearer, closing in for the kill…

15

After a night of little sleep and much restless thought, Calico decided it was time to go on the attack; to try somehow to make contact with Rose Marie Church and dissuade her from her murderous intention. So it was with some consternation – and puzzlement – that she stared at the brown envelopes on top of the pile of morning post. They were addressed in her own hand to Nemesis's box number, but now had the words "Not known at this address" and "Return to sender" scrawled across them. It was all very curious, and in a way more menacing, too. The letters, the first two certainly, had made demands – "publish or die" had been their ultimatum – but this latest development made it clear that no dialogue had been envisaged. Nemesis, it appeared, had no intention of negotiation.

There was one faint possibility: Nina Mallinson. It was clutching at straws, but right now straws were all that Calico had. Nina Mallinson had been Rose Marie Church's agent. Ms McIntyre was sure that the agent was as much in the dark about the author's disappearance as everyone else, but, well, Calico had nothing to lose by asking. Besides, she couldn't think what else to do.

She pressed out the numbers on her phone and listened to the *breep, breep* of the calling tone. A receptionist answered and, after a brief enquiry, put her through to Nina Mallinson's office. A moment or two later the agent's sharp tones sliced down the line.

"This is Calico Dance, Mrs Mallinson, Elizabeth McIntyre's assistant," Calico introduced herself.

The information was not greeted with enthusiasm. "Oh," the agent barked. "Well, what is it you want? I thought Elizabeth and I had said all we had to say to each other last week..."

"This isn't about Marvin Adams," Calico interjected soothingly. "It's about another client of yours – Rose Marie Church." There was a crisp intake of breath at the other end of the line, followed by a heavy exhalation.

"What about Rose Marie Church?" Nina Mallinson asked, in a voice that crackled like burning tinder.

"I wondered if you knew where I might contact her," said Calico.

There was another deep breath before Nina

Mallinson spoke again, this time with cutting precision. "Rose Marie Church is not my client. She hasn't been my client for ten years, since her writing career was ended by your boss and, in a state of utter dejection, she disappeared. I have no idea where she is. Now, if you'll excuse me, I have a long list of *actual* clients to see to."

No sooner had Calico hung up the receiver than she was faced by April Street, whose displeasure was clear even through her dull features.

"I hear that Elizabeth has taken some days off," she said, with obvious disapproval.

"Yes," said Calico. "She needed to get away."

"Don't we all," remarked April tartily. "I'd have thought she might have informed me personally."

"It was a sudden decision," Calico explained. "She's at my aunt's, if you need to speak to her."

April's stony eyes revealed a glimmer of irritation. "I'm sure she'll call *me*, if she needs anything," she remarked, coldly. "She always does." There was no mistaking the animosity in the editor's tone, but whether it was directed at Elizabeth McIntyre or herself, Calico was unsure. One thing was certain, though: April Street couldn't be trusted.

Calico looked once more at the returned letters. It had been her intention to make enquiries about the Nemesis box and see what she could uncover. Romy herself had had a PO box during the six months she'd been away in Rome, so she knew a little about how they worked. You rented a box – usually for a period of a year, Romy thought – at the delivery office which handled your mail. In other words you had to have a permanent address in the same district as your rented box.

Calico had concluded, therefore, that Nemesis actually lived close by. Last night this had seemed like an important discovery and one worth following up, but now that Calico knew the box number wasn't valid, well, Nemesis could be anywhere. Still, it was just about all she had to go on…

After a couple of calls, she got through to the right delivery office. Yes, the woman she spoke to confirmed, P O Box 111 was no longer occupied. It had been held in the name of Rose Marie Church for twenty-two years, but the rental had been cancelled three months ago. The box was now unallocated and mail addressed to it was being returned to sender. Calico listened patiently, greeting this information with a disappointed sigh.

"I really need to get in touch with Miss Church," she said, wistfully. "I wonder, is it possible for you to give me her address?" She posed the question tentatively, expecting an officious refusal, but to her surprise, the woman agreed to her request.

"Yes, I can give you that information," she said, obligingly. "It's not confidential…" Calico heard the woman's fingers tapping on computer keys. "The address I have here is for an agency: Nina Mallinson Literary Agency." She started to give the full address, but Calico stopped her.

"I know the address, thanks," she said. Her mind was whirring, trying to take on board the significance of what she had heard. "In point of fact," the woman continued, "Nina Mallinson is listed here as the box's renter, though the addressee is Rose Marie Church. And it was on the instruction of Nina Mallinson that the rental was cancelled."

"Oh," said Calico. "Thank you."

"You're welcome," said the woman pleasantly, adding as a genial sort of parting shot, "I should say Nina Mallinson's the person to contact if you wish to get in touch with Rose Marie Church."

"Yes," Calico agreed. "I will."

Calico was certain now that Nina Mallinson was hiding something. If she really had had no contact with Rose Marie Church, why had she carried on renting the P O box for the past ten years? And then why cancel it all of a sudden? There were definitely mysteries here that needed unravelling, and to do it, Calico would have to talk again to the waspish agent. But not over the phone this time; it was too easy to be brushed aside. No, this time, she would meet her face to face.

When she told Dan her plan, he insisted on accompanying her.

"You shouldn't go off on your own, Calico," he said, running his hand through his short blond hair. "Things are too dangerous."

"Are you going to protect me, then?" Calico asked provocatively.

"I was thinking more about protecting people *from* you," he replied, his mouth spreading wide in a genial grin. Calico grinned back.

"What about Fred?" she asked, wondering what the gloom-merchant of the post-room would say about his assistant doing a bunk for an hour or so.

"Oh, I'll tell him I had some parcels to collect," Dan said, in the easy lilt that Calico still couldn't trace exactly but was all the more attractive for its elusiveness.

They caught a bus to Nina Mallinson's office and, despite the seriousness of their enterprise, Calico felt strangely light-headed. Dan was a very agreeable companion and the possibility that they might finally be on the brink of a breakthrough in tracking down Nemesis gave her a real buzz that not even the prospect of facing Nina Mallinson could quell.

The agent was in, the receptionist said when they arrived, but she would have to ring through to check that she was free. When she announced Calico's name, the agent's querulous tones barked down the intercom.

"Mrs Mallinson would like to know your business," the receptionist interpreted diplomatically.

"It's a private matter," Calico replied with deliberate vagueness. The receptionist nodded knowingly, then passed on Calico's response. A moment later she pushed a button and looked across at her young visitors.

"Nina Mallinson will see you now," she said,

indicating a door behind them.

"Thank you," said Calico and she exchanged a quick purposeful look with Dan before walking to the door.

Nina Mallinson sat behind a large, old oak desk that made her seem very small. She looked, Calico thought, like a fierce, elderly shrew.

"Thank you for seeing us," she offered politely. But Nina Mallinson was not in the mood for pleasantries.

"You said you had a private matter to discuss," she said curtly. "I can't imagine what it can be, but anyway, sit down, let's hear it. I warn you, though, I'm expecting a client in five minutes' time."

"This won't take long," said Calico affably. She turned towards Dan. "This is Dan Ryan, by the way. He works at Prairie Books, too." Nina Mallinson nodded at Dan, but made no comment. She glanced, pointedly, at her watch.

Calico began by telling the agent all that had happened at Prairie Books over the past week, most of which she already knew. She didn't know, though, about the Nemesis manuscripts and she listened to Calico's brief description of their contents with interest and some incredulity.

"People will do anything to get attention," she said. "You would not believe the offers and threats I have had over the years from would-be authors who believe it my duty to represent them." She screwed up her nose in disdain. "Cranks," she said.

"Nemesis is a crank all right," Calico agreed. "But a very dangerous one. I believe it was Nemesis that murdered Judy Price and is now intending to do the same to Ms McIntyre."

"A little far-fetched, don't you think?" Nina Mallinson suggested dismissively. "But, in any case, I fail to see what all this has to do with me."

Calico took out one of the letters that had been returned to her that morning and passed it across the huge desk.

"Look at the address," she said.

The shock was immediate. Nina Mallinson's small eyes opened wide, her olive skin paled. "But – this number…" she spluttered.

"It's Rose Marie Church's P O box number," Calico stated. Then, after a glance across at Dan to stress his support for her opinion, she said, "We believe that Rose Marie Church *is* Nemesis."

Nina Mallinson gave a perplexed shake of her head. "But that's not possible," she said. "That's simply not possible."

"That's what my aunt thought and Ms McIntyre, too," Calico persisted. "They didn't believe Rose Marie Church could do such things…"

"No," Nina Mallinson interrupted sharply. "You mistake my meaning. I mean that what you suggest is *physically* impossible." She gazed at Calico with searing intensity. "Rose Marie Church is dead."

110

16

So Rose Marie Church wasn't Nemesis after all. But there was a connection somehow, Calico was sure. Nemesis knew about Rose Marie Church, even knew her box number. She was convinced that Nemesis was either someone connected with Rose Marie Church or with Prairie Books – or both. But who? That was the question Dan and Calico asked themselves on the way back to work. Dan expressed suspicion about the agent herself. After all, she had known about the post office box and she certainly had no love for Elizabeth McIntyre.

"But why would she tell us about Rose Marie Church's death?" Calico queried. "If she were guilty, surely she would have continued to keep that secret."

"Maybe," Dan shrugged. "But she didn't tell us the whole truth." His eyes held Calico in a cool, questioning gaze.

"No," Calico agreed. Nina Mallinson had definitely held something back.

She pondered again what the agent had told them. She'd reiterated that for ten years she had heard nothing from Rose Marie Church. She had been a close friend of the author, as well as her agent, and the disappearance had been a devastating blow. She had kept the post office box open in the hope that one day some communication might come through it.

"I could never bring myself to cancel the box," she had explained. "It would have been like admitting that Rose Marie was gone for ever." Then three months ago she had received an anonymous note, informing her that this was indeed the case: Rose Marie Church was dead. As proof, the informant had sent a copy of the author's death certificate: Rose Marie Church had died in County Cork, Ireland, of alcoholic poisoning. Nina Mallinson showed the document to Calico and it certainly appeared to be genuine.

The note had also instructed the agent to keep the author's death secret. It had been Rose Marie Church's wish that her death, like her life during the past decade, should remain unknown. It was the kind of wish that Nina Mallinson would have expected her former client to make and she had intended to satisfy it. It was only astonishment at Calico's accusation that had led her to betray the secret.

But had she really had no communication with the

author in all that time, Calico had pressed – not a word? Did she have no idea why the author had vanished so completely? Was there nothing more she could tell them? It was from this point of the interview that Dan's suspicions arose. For Nina Mallinson had replied that, yes, there was something and for an instant she had seemed on the verge of some new revelation... But suddenly she pursed her lips and became the fierce shrew once more. She had refused to say another word and that was that. The conversation was terminated.

"It's all so complicated," Calico said to Dan now.

"It's that all right," Dan agreed ruefully.

Calico stared out of the window of the bus at the busy city street. There were so many people, so many places to hide, she thought. How could they hope to locate one person among such vastness? And yet, for Elizabeth McIntyre's sake, they had to. They had to discover the identity of Nemesis and prevent the killer from committing any further outrages. *Easier said than done*, Calico thought glumly. At least she had Dan to help her.

As the bus pulled in to yet another stop, Calico's eyes wandered to a café opposite, its bright, red and white striped awning attracting her gaze. She glanced at its clientele idly, her mind still on the conundrum that was Nemesis. Suddenly, her focus sharpened.

"Hey!" she cried and she nudged Dan to get his attention. "Dan, look, that café over there. See the table by the entrance? It's April Street." As she stared, April's companion turned momentarily towards the street and Calico caught a glimpse of a grooved, saggy face, a whiskery ginger-grey beard... "She's with Marvin Adams!"

Dan swivelled in his seat and peered out through the grimy window.

"Are you sure?" he said uncertainly, wiping his hand across the glass. The bus started to pull away.

"Yes," said Calico. "That's definitely April and you can't mistake Marvin Adams!"

"No," said Dan. "I believe you're right."

"I wonder what they're doing together," Calico mused. "I thought Marvin Adams was totally anti Prairie Books."

"Perhaps they're having an affair?" Dan suggested lightly.

Calico pulled a face. "April?" she said incredulously.

"It's possible," said Dan. "Beneath that cool exterior a passionate heart may burn."

"And buses might fly," Calico commented wryly.

But it irked her, this new discovery. Back at work she couldn't help thinking about April. There was something so furtive about her, so inscrutable. Calico wondered just what on earth she was up to. Whose side was she on? She seemed to have a foot in every camp. Though what she hoped to gain from Marvin Adams, Calico couldn't imagine. But seeing April today had stirred some other memory, something that was really bothering Calico. If she could just put her finger on it…

Her reverie was broken by the appearance of Mitch Lennon. He slid over to her desk, with a grin that was more horsy than ever.

"Hi, Calico," he brayed. "Austen needs, like, to see you, you know. In his office, now." Mitch's hair was really lank today and his body gave off an unpleasant, sour odour. It was so bad that Calico almost said something. Somehow, though, she didn't think it would be worth it.

Calico followed Mitch along the corridor towards Austen's office.

"Austen's really, like, peed off, yeah, with the dragon," Mitch informed her. "I reckon she's dead meat."

"Well, that's your opinion," Calico bristled. "Ms McIntyre's very much alive." *And*, she thought determinedly to herself, *she's going to stay that way*.

"Tuh," Mitch uttered, then he looked at Calico and leered. "You fancy, like, going for a drink, after work sometime?" he asked. Fortunately for Calico, at that moment they arrived at the door to Austen Porter's office which saved her from having to make a reply. It did something else, too. It made her recall the last time she'd stood outside this door and the conversation she'd overheard. And in that instant she knew, with a sudden chill, what it was about April that had been bothering her. But she had no time to think about it further, as she followed Mitch into Austen's office.

She was surprised on entering to find not only the sneering editor, but the chairman himself waiting for her. They were seated at a low, round, glass table in the middle of the room, on which stood a Royal Chelsea china teapot and milk jug with four cups and saucers.

"Calico," Austen Porter greeted her gravely. "Have a seat." Calico took the empty seat at the table, while Mitch remained standing like a sentry by the door. The two older men regarded her keenly and, despite herself, Calico couldn't help feeling intimidated: Austen with his thin, sharp face, his eyes small and contemptuous; Dale Jefferson Junior, immaculate in his blue polka-dot bow tie and perfectly pressed pinstripe suit, exuding wealth and power – and easy charm. He smiled now, affably.

"How is Elizabeth?" he asked, pleasantly.

"She's fine, thank you," Calico replied with an uneasy smile.

"Good, good," said Dale Jefferson. "And when might we expect her back, do you know?"

"No, I don't," said Calico. "Soon I should think." *But not too soon*, she thought. *Not until we've found Nemesis.*

"Perhaps you'd pour us some tea, Austen, old chap?" Dale Jefferson drawled in his strangled southern American accent that juxtaposed oddly with the terribly English idiom of his speech. Calico recalled what Romy had said about his desire to be English. She could imagine him sitting out on some village green in the country, sipping his tea as he watched a game of cricket. But his ruthless determination to sell off the company certainly wasn't playing the game.

Dale Jefferson picked up his cup and took a delicate sip of tea. "This deal we are currently negotiating," he floated. "I believe Elizabeth has got quite the wrong idea. She seems to feel rather threatened by it. Would you say that was so?"

"Well, yes, I suppose so," Calico said uncertainly.

"Mmm. That is unfortunate," the chairman continued. "Because I am quite certain, you know, it can only do her good. It would make her a wealthy woman for a start – though I know that is not what most concerns her."

"Elizabeth's a fine editor," Austen Porter noted, although not with huge conviction. Flattery did not come as easily to him, Calico remarked, as to the chairman. "All we ask is that she works *with* us, pulls in the same direction." *Which,* thought Calico, *she'll never do. But, anyway, why are you telling this to me?* Her unspoken question was quickly answered.

"We've been very impressed with you, Calico," said Dale Jefferson, his pink face glowing with warmth, "in the short time you've been with us. You seem to have gained the confidence of Ms McIntyre in a way that few have been able. You have influence beyond your years." He beamed at Calico with the winning, suave smile that had captivated so many women over the years. Calico, however, was quite immune to his charm; she still recalled only too clearly his vicious outburst at Ms McIntyre just a few days ago. "It would be to everyone's advantage," the chairman continued, "if you could persuade Elizabeth to support the proposed merger. It might even be to your aunt's benefit, too. We would be in a position to offer some very lucrative advances to the right authors…" He let this tempting carrot dangle.

"Elizabeth could edit her," Austen added agreeably, but it was an effort, Calico could tell. The customary sneer wasn't far from the surface.

"Think about it," Dale Jefferson proposed. Catching sight of himself in the glass table, he adjusted his bow tie. Then he looked across at Calico. "But think quickly," he said and there was an unmistakable hint of steel in his blue eyes. "We will not wait very long."

17

Calico was angry. She knew Austen and the chairman were trying to use her and it made her mad. As if a few flattering words would win her over: if they thought that, then more fool them. Her loyalty to Elizabeth McIntyre was unquestionable – unlike certain other people at Prairie Books that she could mention. April Street, for example. April who seemed to be in with everyone: Dale Jefferson, Austen Porter, Marvin Adams, Elizabeth McIntyre. She recalled once more that conversation between April and Austen on the night of the lift "accident". She'd presumed that the two had been joking in a snide sort of way when they'd talked of "killing off" Elizabeth McIntyre. But then, this afternoon, she'd remembered the rest of the conversation.

"And why not kill the other off while you're at it," April had suggested with chilly amusement.

"Jude?" Austen had queried and Calico heard again the unpleasant snigger that had followed. *"Well, it's a nice thought, but I'm not sure we'd get away with that, are you?"*

Jude. When Elizabeth McIntyre had told Calico of Judy Price's death, that was the name she'd called her: Jude. Judy Price was *Jude* – and she'd been "killed off", hadn't she? What's more, whoever had murdered her had got away with it – well, so far anyway. The police didn't even think a crime had been committed. But it had, Calico knew that and Nemesis was responsible. Could Austen be Nemesis? she wondered. If Judy Price was opposed to the merger, as Elizabeth McIntyre had said, then he would certainly want her out of the way, wouldn't he, and so would Dale Jefferson. She thought back to her recent meeting with the two men. Could they be in this together? But where and how did April fit in? The more Calico thought about it, the more she believed that April was the key. It was time to confront her...

April wasn't around, though. Her office was empty. Evidently, she hadn't returned yet from her lunch date with Marvin Adams. Calico rang down to Joy to check. Yes, Joy confirmed, April was still out of the building.

"Listen, Joy, could you call up to me as soon as she arrives? I need to speak to her." Then with a casual air, she added, "Oh, I'm in her office, by the way. I've got some labels to do, so I'm borrowing her typewriter." This wasn't exactly the truth, of course, but it wasn't entirely untrue either. She did have some labels to type and it would be easier to bash them out on April's old typewriter rather than set up a document on her PC. Really, though, she wanted to have a look around April's office. She didn't enjoy the deception, but had gone too far now to worry about such minor qualms.

She started with April's desk, opening each drawer in turn and inspecting the contents. It was all very standard stuff: sheets of writing paper, envelopes, spare typewriter ribbons, pens, pencils and other items of stationery; a tube of handcream, a small tub of lip gloss, a little embroidered handkerchief... In one drawer there was a red notebook with jottings that raised Calico's interest for a moment, until she realized they were just words and phrases from manuscripts that needed checking. She sighed with disappointment.

She tried the filing cabinet and found nothing weird or incriminating there either. April was a methodical and experienced editor and her whole room reflected this. It was all very neat and orderly. But, like April herself, what was lacking was warmth, spark. There was nothing personal or distinctive: there were no plants or flowers, no pictures or knick-knacks. The one revealing thing in the room was a photograph, on her desktop, of April herself with a golden labrador. Calico stared at the photograph for a moment or two then sighed again: finding out anything about April beyond the fact that she was a dog-lover seemed impossible. She made no tracks. Fleetingly the thought passed through Calico's mind that maybe there wasn't anything *to* discover, but then, if that were so, she told herself, why all these secretive meetings? April had to be up to something.

Bright sunshine gushed into the room, spilling over the desktop and its meagre spread of objects: the almost empty filing trays, the diary, the typewriter... For a moment, sitting at April's desk, Calico was back in her study room, in the early summer, a schoolgirl with a textbook and notebook in front of her, doing her final revision notes before the exams, her head full of historical facts, French grammar, mathematical formulae – academic things. It seemed such a long time ago, yet it was only a matter of weeks. And here she was, an editorial assistant in a publishing house, trying to uncover a murderer and save her boss's life... It was incredible, like something out of a story. But the tension she felt in her stomach right now was no fiction. What was happening was deadly real.

Her eyes focused on April's typewriter. Half thinking she might type those labels she needed after all, she dragged the black machine across the desk towards her. It sat in a beam of sunlight now that illuminated the typewriter ribbon, highlighting the words imprinted there. Calico froze. Hands still outstretched holding the typewriter, eyes fixed on the ribbon, she sat and stared. Among the line of letters, three words leapt out at her – two distinctive words she had read the night before and another that she had read several times during the last fortnight. "Bloody reckoning", she read and then "Nemesis". Putting down the label, she opened the top of the typewriter with trembling fingers and removed the ribbon cartridge. Then she held the ribbon up to the light and examined it closely. There was no doubt about it. The letter that had arrived at Elizabeth McIntyre's flat the previous day had been typed on this machine!

Her heart thumped hard and fast. Then missed a beat as she realized the office door was opening. Looking across tensely, she saw April Street in the doorway, her face a mask of stone.

"What exactly are you doing?" April asked, coldly.

Calico glanced down at the ribbon in her hands. "I – well –" she stammered, flustered for an instant.

"Yes?" April queried sharply.

Calico swallowed. She took a breath to try to compose herself. Then she fixed April with a steady gaze.

"I've just discovered that you've been sending Elizabeth McIntyre threatening letters," she said, with a coolness she didn't feel. "You're Nemesis, aren't you?"

April's android-like features remained impassive. There was just the slightest twitch of the mouth as she gently pushed the door shut behind her and moved into the room. Calico eyed the closed door anxiously, feeling suddenly vulnerable, alone.

"I don't honestly see what business it is of yours what I do," April said, in a voice of ice. She was standing right in front of Calico now, with just the desk between them.

"I'm Ms McIntyre's assistant and someone's trying to kill her," Calico said simply. "Right now, I think it's you."

April allowed herself the luxury of a smile, but from the mouth only, her deep grey eyes two unyielding stones.

"If I'd wanted to kill Elizabeth McIntyre, I'd have done it before now, don't you think?" she remarked.

Calico pursed her lips, her mouth felt suddenly very dry. "I – don't know," she said uncertainly. "All I know is that Elizabeth McIntyre received a threatening letter yesterday and it was typed on this machine. The print is still here on this ribbon." Calico held up the ribbon cartridge towards April.

April's thin eyebrows raised slightly. "Typing a letter is hardly the same thing as trying to kill someone," she pointed out critically, as though mentally putting a blue pencil line through Calico's words. "Imagination is no substitute for logical thought." She sounded just like a teacher – a teacher on the verge of giving out a detention.

"You did type this letter, though?" Calico said, adopting a similarly tough tone.

"Yes," said April. "But I still fail to see what business it is of yours."

"You threatened to kill Ms McIntyre," Calico

accused.

April snorted. "I did no such thing. I just stated a few home truths, that's all."

"You said she'd receive a bloody reckoning. That was a threat, wasn't it?" Calico pressed. "And what about all those other things you wrote in the other letters."

Shallow wrinkles appeared on April's smooth forehead. "What other letters?" she queried. "I only wrote two."

"There have been five Nemesis letters," Calico insisted.

"Five?"

"Yes," said Calico. Briefly she recalled the five letters and roughly what each contained. April's frown deepened.

"I've only sent two letters," she reiterated. "It was after you showed me that first letter that the idea came to me. I recognized the box number. It was the same box number as the one used by an author we used to deal with many years ago – Rose Marie Church, another of Elizabeth's casualties."

"I know all about Rose Marie Church," Calico said quickly.

"I doubt it," said April. "Not if you've just heard Elizabeth's version. She axed Rose Marie Church, just like she's axed other authors over the years when they failed to be useful to her, just like she's axed Marvin Adams – though goodness knows in his case it was about time. When authors most need her editorial support and expertise, she withdraws it. She only tolerates authors as long as they make her look good. Elizabeth's a glory-seeker, you see, she always has been and selfish, too. She only does what is good for her. What I said in my letters was true."

"Then why did you tell me not to show the first letter to Ms McIntyre?" Calico asked.

"I thought I could do a better job," April said clinically. "That letter wouldn't have worried Elizabeth. So I thought I'd write my own, make it sound as if it really might have come from Rose Marie Church. I wanted to shake her up."

The explanation had a ring of truth to it, Calico had to admit. There was a marked disparity in style and tone between the Nemesis letters that Calico had opened and the ones Elizabeth McIntyre had received personally. It struck Calico now as obvious that they were written by different hands. But there was more to incriminate April in the recent crimes than just those letters.

"That Friday night," Calico said, "the night the lift was sabotaged, I heard you and Austen talking. You were discussing killing off Ms McIntyre and Judy Price." April's large, dull eyes flickered for an instant with astonishment.

"That's absurd," she said with unusual vehemence.

Calico pressed home her attack. "I was right outside the door of Austen's office," she insisted. "'*Why don't we kill off Jude?*' you said. I heard you."

April's expression altered now from surprise to contempt.

"What you heard," she said frostily, "was Austen and I having a *literary* discussion. We were talking about Thomas Hardy. I take it you've heard of Thomas Hardy?"

"Of course I have," Calico said with feeling.

"Then you'll know that two of his best-known books are *Jude the Obscure* and *Tess of the D'Urbervilles*." She paused just long enough for Calico to nod. "Well, they happen to be two of the chairman's favourite books. He wants to publish them on a new classics list when the merger goes through. Austen doesn't. He thinks Hardy's novels are sensationalist and overrated. I happen to agree with him. You don't, I suppose."

"No, I don't," Calico confirmed. "I studied *Tess* for English A-level and I loved it."

"Well, you're only a kid, aren't you?" April said, with a sneer that could have come straight from the face of Austen Porter himself. But Calico refused to be fazed. She returned April's stare with interest.

"I may be a kid," she said. "But at least I'm loyal. I don't desert my friends when they most need me."

April wrinkled her long nose. "You don't understand anything," she said. "Elizabeth's the disloyal one, not me. I'm not trying to bring down the company."

"She's standing for what she believes in," Calico persisted.

"And what's that?" April scoffed. "Rubbish like *The Embryo Clinic.*"

"It isn't rubbish. It's a good book," Calico replied with passion. An image appeared in her head of the author and April Street in the café. "I thought you and Marvin Adams were friends," she said more calmly.

April studied Calico with cold amusement. "Whatever gave you that idea?" she said.

"I saw you together, this lunchtime," said Calico.

At this revelation the mask slipped and April's grey eyes opened wide with surprise. "What is this!" she gasped with rare emotion. "Are you spying on me?"

"No," said Calico and she quickly explained how she came to make her discovery.

"Well," said April tartly. "You've got it wrong — again. Marvin Adams thought I might be able to help him. He asked me to meet him for lunch. So I did. I told him that Elizabeth was on her way out, which seemed to give him some satisfaction."

"And you led him to believe that you were on his side, I suppose, like you've done with everyone else," Calico said toughly. "Well, whose side are you really on, April? That's what I'd like to know."

April's small mouth puckered with bitterness. "Would you?" she said. "And who the hell are you? What do you know about anything? You think Elizabeth's the heroine and I'm the villain — the rat deserting a sinking ship. You think I've let Elizabeth down, betrayed her. Well, let me tell you, Elizabeth doesn't give a fig about me. Did she ever ask my opinion about the merger? Does she ever ask my opinion about anything? No. I'm just her lackey, the one who does all the things she doesn't want to do herself. Takes care of all the nitty-gritty details, the hands-on editing, while she wallows in glory... At least she used to discuss things with me. But now, it seems, she'd rather talk to you – a kid she's known barely a week. Well, I've had enough. Now I'm looking out for myself. I'm not going to be tied to Elizabeth any more. If she wants to destroy her career, that's her decision. I'm staying at Prairie Books."

"So that's why you've been meeting with Austen Porter behind her back?" Calico flung.

April was unmoved. "Elizabeth's finished," she said, flatly, her face an inexpressive mask once more. "And it's her own doing. You know, I wouldn't be at all surprised if she sent those other Nemesis letters to herself. She'd stop at nothing to scupper this merger." The chairman, Calico recalled had intimated something similar, and she gave April no more credence. They hadn't been there in the lift that night, had they? They hadn't seen the state she was in. If Calico hadn't rescued her, she'd have died. No one would go to those lengths to spite a business deal.

"You can't trust Elizabeth, Calico," April said, interrupting Calico's thoughts with a voice that was almost sympathetic. "You mustn't let her take you in. She'll use you, just like she used me." This surprisingly solicitous caution delivered, April's face resumed its android quality. "Now, if you don't mind," she said, coolly, "I'd like my office back."

18

"I'm really sorry, Calico," Joy apologized for not informing her of April's arrival in the building. "She must have come in when I went to the loo and Fred was on reception. I was only away a few minutes…"

Calico smiled. "It's OK, Joy," she assured her friend. "It worked out fine. I needed to talk to April anyway."

At that instant, Dan appeared. "So you've been talking to April," he said good-humouredly. "Have you uncovered her secrets?" Calico gave him a wry grin.

"Well, a few of them," she said. "She doesn't like me for a start." She shook her head. "Do you know, I really think she's jealous of me. She thinks Ms McIntyre thinks more of me than she does of her."

"Well, *we* certainly do," said Dan, raising one eyebrow in mock flirtation. "Don't we, Joy?"

"Absolutely," Joy confirmed with a sparkling smile.

"Yeah, well, you guys are crazy," Calico said, dismissively.

She told Joy and Dan about her conversation with April.

"So Elizabeth's got no ally there then," Dan remarked when she'd finished.

Calico pushed a stray lock of hair from her forehead.

"No way," she said vehemently. "She's in Austen's camp. At least, I think she is. It's hard to be sure of anything with April. We're going to have to watch her, though – that I am sure about."

"Along with everyone else," Dan added. "Maybe they're all in it together." His eyes widened dramatically. "A plot to remove wicked Elizabeth McIntyre."

"I can't believe that," said Joy. She gave Calico an earnest look. "What do you think, Calico?"

Calico shrugged. "I don't know," she sighed. "Every discovery seems to make things more complicated. Someone's got it in for Ms McIntyre, though, I'm sure of that. And, whoever it is, we've got to stop them."

The end of the working day couldn't come soon enough for Calico. It had been a momentous day and she felt quite exhausted by all its confrontations and revelations. And it wouldn't stop either, she knew, when she got home – not with Elizabeth McIntyre there. For the first time, she actually wished she had a place of her own. She wished too that she had a friend outside all of this that she could talk to, but what had happened over the past couple of weeks was just too weird, she felt, for any of her old school-friends to comprehend. It was such a huge leap from her old life; it was as if she had walked on to another planet. She did want company of her own age, though, so on the spur of the moment, she invited Dan and Joy to come round for dinner, thinking their presence would help to make things less intense back home. But neither could make it.

"I've got a drama class," Joy apologized. "I'd miss it, only it's me that's running it!"

"And I promised I'd run an errand for my mum," Dan said a little sheepishly. "But, maybe some other time?" His green eyes drew her in like the sea.

"Sure," she said casually. Secretly, though, she was looking forward to the prospect already.

She travelled home in a dream, going through everything that had occurred that day: finding out about the post office box, the meeting with Nina Mallinson and the discovery that Rose Marie Church was dead, seeing April and Marvin Adams together, the interview with Austen Porter and the chairman, the showdown with April Street... She'd stirred up all kinds of bees it seemed, without getting any nearer to the nest. There was so much to take in, to consider... *"Read, mark, learn and inwardly digest."* For a second or two before she placed them, the words floated about in her head. Then she shivered and took a deep breath. Rose Marie Church may be dead, but Nemesis was out there somewhere, waiting to strike...

Maybe it was this chilling thought that was the cause, but as she walked the last few hundred metres from the tube station to Romy's flat in the fading daylight, she was touched by a feeling of unease. This feeling grew as she got further from the bustle and noise of the busy main road and into the small street where the flat was. She had the distinct sense that she was being followed. At one point, she heard footsteps and turned quickly to see a boy and a dog moving away down another street. She sighed with relief, chastising herself for being so silly. Then she walked on.

She was just metres from the small apartment block that housed Romy's flat, when she heard renewed footsteps behind her. She turned again, more slowly this time, out of curiosity rather than fear. But fear soon came. For when she looked back along the dusky street, it was empty; there was no sign of anyone. She listened intently for a few instants, hoping to hear the squeak of a back-door gate or the slam of a front door that would provide some innocent explanation.

The street, though, was completely, eerily, almost maliciously silent. Prickles ran up her neck. Her stomach seemed to drop away, as panic began to rise within her. She twisted round and fled towards the flat, convinced as she did that she could hear running footsteps pursuing her.

Sweating, she arrived at the big front door of the apartment block, throwing herself against it as she fumbled for her key. It seemed to take an eternity to draw it from her pocket. At last, though, it was in her hand, between her fingers, in the lock... She shoved open the door and fell inside, hearing the door swish slowly, then click shut behind her. Anxiously she glanced around and was relieved to see she was alone in the hallway.

For some moments, she could hardly breathe. She leaned back against the wall, doubled-over, panting. Then the door to Romy's flat opened and Elizabeth McIntyre appeared.

"Calico?" she said, puzzled. "Are you all right? What's the matter?"

Calico gestured towards the front door. "There was ... someone ... following me," she uttered between gasps.

"Someone following you?" said Elizabeth McIntyre. Before Calico could say a word, the older woman had marched past her to the front door and yanked it open. A tepid breeze drifted into the hallway.

"There's no one there now," Elizabeth McIntyre declared in a tone that, to Calico anyway, seemed to suggest a doubt that there ever had been anyone.

Indeed, she was starting to doubt it herself. But the doubts didn't last long. Only as long as it took to look down and catch sight of the piece of paper lying on the mat. Shakily, Calico picked it up.

"*'YOU HAD THE CHANCE TO PUBLISH, NOW YOU DIE. THE FLY FLOP OF VENGEANCE SHALL BEAT YOU TO PIECES. I SHALL BE REVENGED FOR ALL'*," she read aloud in a quiet, flat voice. The bright pink that, just instants before, had been in her face as a result of her running, had all faded, leaving her complexion unusually pale. In trembling hands, she held the paper out for Elizabeth McIntyre to take.

"It's from Nemesis," she said.

19

The evening was dominated by Nemesis. Calico brought Romy and Elizabeth McIntyre up to date with the day's extraordinary events that had ended so traumatically, and they had disturbing news of their own. Earlier in the day, while Elizabeth McIntyre was resting, Romy had received a phone call from Prairie Books requesting that the editor should come in later that afternoon for a meeting with the chairman. When her guest had appeared, Romy had passed on the message. Elizabeth McIntyre had been on the point of leaving when there was another phone call – again from Prairie Books. This time it was Dale Jefferson himself, enquiring after the health of his distinguished editor and asking when he might expect her back at work. There were things that required urgent discussion he said. He was quite taken aback to be informed that Elizabeth McIntyre was about to leave for Prairie Books that very minute to attend a meeting that he himself had arranged. He had no knowledge of any such meeting, he said. In fact, he had another meeting away from the office and would not be returning that day…

"Nemesis," Calico said to her boss. "It was Nemesis, trying to trick you into going back."

"And very nearly succeeding," Romy added.

"He's determined to get you," Calico agreed, grimly.

"He?" Ms McIntyre queried.

"Or she," Calico conceded. She glanced at her aunt. "Was it a man or a woman on the phone, Romy?"

"It was a woman," Romy said. "Your receptionist."

"Joy?"

"Yes, Joy, that's it. Joy Sparrow." She frowned. "Sparrow," she repeated, her large, green eyes narrowing thoughtfully. The others regarded her expectantly.

"What is it, Romy?" Calico prompted.

Romy's eyes widened once more. "Oh, it was just the name, Sparrow," she said. "I knew it rang a bell." She paused briefly before continuing. "Sparrow was Rose Marie Church's real name."

Lying back a little later in a warm, bubbly bath,

Calico considered this latest revelation and what it might mean. Were Joy and Rose Marie Church related somehow? Neither Romy or Elizabeth McIntyre seemed to think this likely. It was well known that Rose Marie Church was an only child, Elizabeth McIntyre told Calico. It was an important aspect of her work: all the heroines in her books were only children and suffered in some way because of it. She herself had been badly affected as a child by her parents' break-up: her father had walked out and Rose Marie Church hated him for it – the reason she had taken her mother's maiden name in adult life. As far as they knew, she had never married herself or had any children.

"We can't be sure about that, though," Calico had stressed. "If no one ever saw her, she could have had a child and kept it secret." She had to admit, though, that the idea was rather far-fetched. Still, she was niggled by the Sparrow thing. It was another coincidence. But supposing Joy and Rose Marie Church were related. What could that mean? That Joy was Nemesis? The suggestion was absurd. And yet... She *had* phoned to set up a bogus meeting between the chairman and Ms McIntyre. And Joy more than anyone had opportunity on her side. She could easily have started the fire, for example. But then, Calico reminded herself, Joy had been Nemesis's first victim, hadn't she? She'd hardly send herself a letter bomb and risk doing herself serious injury. She could have been maimed for life. And yet (there it was again, that restless shadow of suspicion), well, she hadn't been. In fact, her injuries had been very minor – surprisingly minor. What's more, she'd been really keen to get straight back to work. And, of course, Joy *was* an actress by profession. She surely, more than anyone, could carry off deception…

No, it was ridiculous. Calico's meandering thoughts ran into a cul-de-sac. She simply couldn't believe it – not of Joy. Joy was her friend, everyone's friend. Calico closed her eyes and tried to give herself up to the warm foamy water, to let it soothe away the heaviness that clung to her like clay. For half an hour she soaked, but the troubled waters in her head would not be quietened. There were so many loose ends, so many possible suspects: Austen Porter, Dale Jefferson, April Street, Nina Mallinson and now Joy…

Calico's head was spinning with it all. But one thing seemed clear: dead or not, Rose Marie Church was involved in this affair somehow. She was the key. There was nothing random about Nemesis using the same box number as the deceased author. No, *that* was planned, she felt sure. Somebody wanted Elizabeth McIntyre to make the connection. But if this was a case of revenge, why wait so long? Why wait till after she was dead? And, anyway, if every author who had a manuscript rejected decided to kill their editor, there'd be no editors left, would there? There had to be more to it than just rejection, surely.

Could someone be using the Rose Marie Church connection for their own ends – Austen Porter, for example? April's explanation of her conversation with Austen on the night of the lift incident had been plausible enough, but still Calico didn't trust her. She had to admit, though, that it was one heck of a story to invent at the drop of a hat. But then that was the thing about all that had happened over the last week or so: it was hard to find the border between truth and fiction. At times, indeed, it was as if it didn't exist.

After her bath, Calico found Romy sitting up alone in the sitting-room, reading. Elizabeth McIntyre had retired to bed. Calico saw that the book her aunt was holding was *Men Beware Women*.

"I thought I'd give it another read," Romy said. "It's a long time since I read it. It holds up still, I think."

Calico nodded. "I enjoyed it," she said. She pulled her hair back and secured it with a scrunchie. "Well, if enjoy's the right word," she added with a small grimace.

"Mmm, it is rather bloody," Romy agreed.

Calico glanced at the book in Romy's hands and took in again the picture of Rose Marie Church on the back cover. As before, the eyes leapt out at her. She sighed.

"I wish I'd met her," she said wistfully. "She looks so interesting."

Romy pursed her lips. "Yes," she said, "Rose

Marie was certainly that. I still find it hard to take in that she's dead." For a few moments, aunt and niece sat in pensive, motionless silence, then Calico looked over at Romy.

"Romy," she said. "Look, I know this might sound a bit of a cheek and do say if you think so, but, well, do you think I could have a look at those letters Rose Marie Church sent you? I just feel like I need to know her. She's so much at the centre of everything that's going on."

Romy quickly allayed Calico's fears of giving offence. "Of course," she said. "Be my guest. Rose Marie was such a fine letter writer. Her letters deserve to be read. You may find them a little shocking on occasions…"

Calico smiled. "Don't worry," she said, with a light toss of her head, "after all that's happened this past week, I don't think anything could shock me."

"You'd be surprised," Romy said with the heavy voice of experience. Calico shrugged and departed.

It took her a while to find the letters. The wardrobe was big and though everything was in a kind of order, it required some searching. Calico eventually located the pile of Rose Marie Church correspondence at the back of the second shelf down, gathered together with a large elastic band. She pulled out the pile and, putting them on the bed, removed the fastening, so that the letters fanned out over the counterpane. Then she sat down to read.

It was fascinating stuff. The letters were written

over a period of a couple of years and they revealed a woman with an appealing sense of humour and profound intelligence. At least, the earlier ones did. But as Calico worked her way down to the bottom of the pile, the humour grew blacker and what came over was an increasingly dark view of human nature. There was a kind of desperation, a feeling of betrayal and alienation about the final letters that made them hard to read. It was like watching someone suffer torture. Romy, it seemed, was one of the few people the author trusted – although towards the end, it seemed, even she had slipped in the volatile author's affections. Rose Marie Church seemed at times to resent her. In one place, she attacked Romy's writing as being too refined, *bloodless* – hardly a criticism that could be levelled at her own work, Calico reflected. Later on in the same letter, however, Rose Marie Church praised Romy as "one of the very best living writers of historical fiction". Marvin Adams was another author upon whom Rose Marie obviously depended. His name came up frequently, to such an extent indeed that Calico wondered whether there might have been some romantic attachment. After all, hadn't Romy said that he was just about the only person she met with in person? They were very close in any case, that much was obvious.

By the time Calico reached the bottom of the pile, she felt quite exhausted. Reading Rose Marie Church's letters was like reading a particularly intense novel. There was no idle gossip, no easy chit-chat, no

143

wasting of words in simple pleasantries. She was, Calico conjectured, a woman on the edge. It was no surprise that she had toppled over. It was still puzzling, though, why she had decided to cut herself off as she had. OK, Romy had been away when the Prairie Books rejection had happened, but what about Marvin Adams? Hadn't he been around? Why didn't she turn to him? Why had she vanished so completely? Where had she gone?

Calico yawned. Glancing at the clock, she saw it was well after midnight and, suddenly, she became aware of the deep darkness outside. It was time for bed. Yawning again, she tidied the letters into a pile once more and then replaced the elastic band. She returned the pile to its place at the back of the shelf in the wardrobe. But it wouldn't go. Something was obstructing it. Calico stretched her arm out and up to reach the back of the shelf. Her hand found something – a small wad of envelopes that it seemed had slipped down from the shelf above.

She drew them out and looked at them. There were three letters, all addressed to Romy in Rose Marie Church's handwriting. But the odd thing was that none of them appeared to have been opened.

Calico found Romy still in the sitting-room, reading. It took her an instant or so to take in what Calico was saying, but then she nodded with comprehension.

"They must have come when I was in Rome," she said, studying the envelopes. "I told you I stopped writing to Rose Marie. Well, I decided when I was in Rome that I wouldn't read any more of her letters either. They'd become too painful, disturbing. I must have just put these in the wardrobe unopened." She shrugged. "How strange to think they've lain there all this time…" She looked at the letters with a troubled air.

"Aren't you going to open them?" Calico prompted eagerly. "They could be really important."

Romy frowned. "I don't know," she said quietly. "To be honest, it rather gives me the creeps."

"Well, would you prefer me to read them first?" Calico offered.

Romy pursed her lips, then nodded quickly. "Yes," she said. "You read them."

Romy got up and poured herself a large brandy, while Calico sat down on the sofa and read. The first two letters were similar in tone and content to those she'd recently finished reading. They were full of bitterness, disillusion, abuse and accusation – Prairie Books had dropped her and she had nothing but angry contempt for Elizabeth McIntyre. Some of the names she called her made the attacks by the chairman and Austen Porter seem mild by comparison. And the editor wasn't the only one to get a lashing. Romy was rebuked fiercely for failing to write and even Marvin Adams, apparently, had fallen out of favour. In Rose Marie Church's eyes, he was now "a worthless leech".

If all of this was explosive, it was nothing to the

drama of the final letter. It was written in a legible but unsteady hand, as if in a state of great emotion, which, on reading the letter's brief contents, Calico quickly realized must have been the case. Her eyes bulged with astonishment as they scanned the few, extraordinary sentences on the page in her hands. "This torment," Calico read, "is my punishment. I am being punished for my crime. I gave away my child and now I am cursed for it. I must find my child. Only my child can save me. I must go and reclaim my child. I cannot live without my child. My child! He made me give away my child! May he be cursed for ever. May you all be cursed for ever. I live only now for my child." The letter ended with a signature that was a wild scrawl.

Silently, Calico handed the letter to her aunt. As Romy read, her eyes too widened in amazement. Then she turned to her niece. "My God," she murmured. The two stared at one another in bewildered incredulity.

"I was wrong," Calico uttered at last. "I can still be shocked."

Romy frowned and her lip trembled. "Rose Marie had a child," she said hoarsely. "And she gave it away." She fell into the nearest armchair. "Poor Rose Marie. Poor, poor Rose Marie," she moaned.

20

Calico woke late after a night of fitful sleep and disturbing dreams that left her feeling weary and fuzzy-headed. Shuffling out into the sitting-room, yawning, she was met by the sight of Elizabeth McIntyre, immaculately groomed and about to leave. She was dressed in a smart black suit and a cream silk blouse; silver zigzag earrings dangled from her lobes and her work bag was clasped in one hand. She loomed before Calico like a vision: dazzling, sexy, magnificent.

"Where are you going?" Calico asked, groggily.

"I'm going to work," her boss replied with her customary brusqueness. Calico opened her mouth to protest but Elizabeth McIntyre held up an imperious hand. "I've got to go back, Calico," she said. "I can't stay here any longer. I'm just putting you and Romy in danger." She drew herself up, bristling. "I'm a big girl. I can fight my own battles. If this Nemesis wants to destroy me, well, let them try. I'll be ready. I can look after myself."

The thought of Elizabeth McIntyre back at Prairie Books didn't exactly fill Calico with joy; it would make her such an accessible target to whoever it was that wanted to get rid of her. But Calico could see her boss's point. She couldn't hide away in Romy's flat for ever. And besides, that wasn't Ms McIntyre's way. If there was a problem, she confronted it. It was one of the many things Calico admired about her. And maybe this was the best way to get Nemesis to show him-or-herself. It was the potentially fatal out-come, though, that concerned Calico. But at least before Elizabeth McIntyre left, Calico managed to draw an assurance from her that she wouldn't go up to the reference library, and that if anyone asked her to, she would immediately contact Calico or Dan.

She didn't mention Joy. Until last night, she would have, but now she wasn't sure. It was hard to believe anything bad of Joy and yet the revelations of the evening before planted suspicions in Calico's mind that her friend might not be quite the open book she appeared. Rose Marie Church had had a child and Joy could well be it. She was around the right age, she had the right surname. And if she were the daughter of Rose Marie Church – or Sparrow – then she also had a very good reason for hating Elizabeth McIntyre. In such circumstances, she could hardly be entrusted with trying to protect her.

Of course, it was always possible that Rose Marie Church hadn't had a child at all. Her words in that final letter might have been no more than the rantings of a woman plunging into madness. But Calico had an idea how to find out. As soon as she was dressed, she phoned Nina Mallinson. She told the agent about the letter they had discovered and its shocking revelation. The secret was out, she said.

Her statement was met by a lengthy silence and she was worried briefly that the agent was going to hang up on her. But she didn't. She sighed heavily, then admitted that she had known about the child. It was this that she had been near to disclosing to Calico and Dan the day before. Rose Marie Church had had a child twenty-two years ago. The child had been adopted at birth. At first she'd wanted to keep the child, but as her pregnancy progressed she became very depressed and believed she would not be a fit mother.

"What about the father?" Calico asked.

"The father didn't want the child at all," Nina Mallinson replied, with more than a hint of disapproval. "He wanted Rose Marie to have an abortion."

Something clicked in Calico's brain. "The father, it was Marvin Adams, wasn't it?"

The agent exhaled sharply. "Yes, it was Marvin Adams," she confirmed. "You seem to know everything."

"No," said Calico. "I don't know the identity of the child. I don't even know if it was a boy or a girl."

"No more do I," Nina Mallinson said, regretfully. "I don't believe Rose Marie Church knew herself."

Up to this point, the agent had been surprisingly cooperative, but that stopped as soon as Calico expressed interest in contacting Marvin Adams. He had gone away to a secret location to rest and recover from the shock of being dropped by Prairie Books, she informed Calico. She had no idea when he would return and she had no intention of revealing his whereabouts to Calico or anyone else. She had revealed too much already, she said. And that was that; Calico could get no more out of her. But that was OK. She'd found out what she'd needed to know.

Of course, there was always a possibility that Marvin Adams was Nemesis and might at this very moment be planning to strike out at Elizabeth McIntyre. If he had loved Rose Marie Church then he had no doubt been devastated by her disappearance. He'd have known too how badly Prairie Books' rejection had affected her. Now he too had been rejected...

He had to be angry, surely, and resentful, and, as his past record showed, he could be moved to violent action: he had killed before. Maybe he could be driven to kill again...

She recalled his meeting with April Street. What if, instead of giving Adams the brush-off as she had claimed, April was actually his inside accomplice?

Certainly she had no desire to protect Ms McIntyre. Quite the contrary. All this was conjecture, though: a heap of *maybes* and *what ifs*. What Calico needed was a decisive blow to split this seemingly impenetrable rock apart. And maybe, just maybe, the discovery that Rose Marie Church had had a child was it.

She got into work as quickly as possible and was relieved to see Elizabeth McIntyre in her office, cup of stewed coffee in front of her, glasses on, poring over a manuscript and looking composed. For the moment, then, she was safe enough, but for how long? It was time, Calico decided, to visit the scene of the proposed crime, to start preparing herself for the attack, she felt sure, was soon to happen. She walked away down the corridor to the stairs, then climbed quickly to the top floor.

The reference library, as usual, was deserted. In her fortnight at Prairie Books, this was the first time Calico had been up there. From conversations she'd had with other employees, she'd gathered that the reference library was regarded as something of a McIntyre folly. It was she who had insisted on its installation, mainly to find a home for the huge collection of other publishers' books that were cluttering up the editorial department. "Reference library", however, was rather a grand term for what was basically a dumping ground – as Calico could now see for herself. There *were* rows of shelves and units, neatly lined with books, but below and around them was a jumble of other things: piles of old magazines and newspapers; pieces of broken furniture; discarded typewriters and word processors; untidy heaps of box files; a couple of dented, paint-chipped, metal filing cabinets. Calico could easily understand why no one wanted to spend time in here. Just finding a chair intact enough to sit on would be difficult.

She made her way through the room, looking about her, peering into any nooks and crannies – not that she expected to find anything. She just wanted to get to know the place, to make sure that if the worst did come to the worst and somehow Nemesis did manage to trick Elizabeth McIntyre into coming up here that she would know the terrain. Standing in the middle of the room, she was overwhelmed by an atmosphere of menace. It struck her suddenly with chilling certainty that Nemesis would be here, in this room, in the very near future – already had been perhaps, checking out the place like she was now. She tried to imagine the scene, but she couldn't. The identity of Nemesis was as perplexing a mystery as ever: she had no picture of the murderer, she didn't even know the sex. Nemesis had always been ahead, setting the pace, pulling the strings. As she glanced about her, a feeling of deep foreboding filled her stomach, telling her that this room would indeed be the final battleground...

Feeling a little claustrophobic in that cluttered, stuffy room, she walked over to the window and opened it. She stared out over the world beyond –

the great, wide, sprawling world she had been hurled into. It seemed wild, unruly, amoral, dangerous, exciting. A place where friendships were dispensable, loyalty easily exchangeable, where people killed for – for what? *That* was the question. This was the real world and she was part of it.

Leaning over the sill she took a deep breath and another, looking down past the black fire-escape ladder that trailed down the wall of the building to the ground far below. Shivering a little now, she drew back inside. She took a last glance about the room, then walked to the door. As she went out, she noticed that there was an alarm pad at one side of the door. The bulb wasn't alight, so the alarm, she presumed, wasn't on. But it set her thinking. What if it were to be switched on? And left on?

When she got to her desk she called up Fred.

"Ms McIntyre has asked me to ask you to set the alarm on the reference library," she said. "Someone's been taking her books."

"They're welcome to them," Fred grumbled. "That place is a disgrace. Imagine if I let the shed get into a state like that."

"Perhaps you should take charge of it," Calico suggested.

Fred tutted. "I've got quiet enough responsibilities of my own, young lady," he said, "without sorting out the affairs of you editors."

"But you will set the alarm?" Calico asked, beseechingly.

"Hmm, all right," Fred agreed. "But it'll be on Ms McIntyre's head if someone sets it off and the police are called."

"Of course, Fred, absolutely," Calico said reassuringly, remarking to herself grimly that Fred didn't realize how apt his caution was: it would indeed be on Ms McIntyre's head.

Later, she went down to the post-room to find Dan and bring him up to date with everything that had happened since she'd last seen him. His blue-green eyes grew very serious when she told him of her stalking by Nemesis on the way home the night before and showed him the note he had left her.

"'*The fly flop of vengeance shall beat you to pieces. I shall be revenged for all*'," he read.

"More from *The Revenger's Tragedy*, I presume," Calico remarked grimly.

Dan nodded. "It certainly sounds like it," he agreed. "It seems as if no one's safe. You should mind your step, Calico." At his expression of concern, Calico felt a glow of pleasure that dispersed, momentarily, the icy tension that had started to grip her.

"Don't worry, I shall," she responded with a faint smile.

Calico told Dan about her conversation with Nina Mallinson that morning. The news made a suitably big impression. Dan looked quite stunned. His eyes seemed to stare right through Calico, as he said with quiet intensity, "I knew Nina Mallinson was holding something back. I bet she could tell us a lot more if she wanted to…" His gaze dropped, softened. "So Marvin Adams is the father of Rose Marie Church's child," he said, pensively.

"Yes," said Calico. "He probably has no idea, though, who the child is. Not if he didn't have any contact with Rose Marie after she disappeared." She hesitated for a moment, then looking Dan in the eyes, she went on, "I think I know who the child is."

Dan's gaze slid sharply into focus. His normally open face closed up in a freckly frown. "Tell me," he said.

"Rose Marie Church's real name was Sparrow," Calico offered.

"Sparrow!" Dan exclaimed. "You mean…" He listened intently to Calico's thoughts about Joy and the possible evidence against her – circumstantial all of it, she stressed, but there nonetheless.

"I think I should talk to her at lunchtime," she said. "Could you cover the phones for a while?"

"Sure," Dan agreed. "Sure."

"Thanks, Dan," Calico said warmly. Then flashing him her most alluring smile, she added, "I'm really glad I can count on you."

Calico returned to her department just in time to witness April Street emerging from Elizabeth McIntyre's office, her face as inexpressive as ever. She didn't acknowledge Calico, simply walked past in the direction of Austen Porter's office. Calico knocked on her boss's door.

"Is everything OK, Ms McIntyre?" she enquired.

Elizabeth McIntyre's expression was serenity itself. "Yes, everything's fine, thanks, Calico," she replied calmly. "I think April and I understand one another quite clearly now." The editor's serenity was tinged with steel; she was back to her formidable self. "Dale and Austen have summoned me to a lunch meeting to discuss the Prairie Books situation," she continued. "Apparently the deadline for the merger deal is tomorrow." She smiled mischievously. "I suppose they intend one last attempt to persuade me to give up my opposition. With Judy gone, they have to have my approval. They won't get it, of course, but still…" She pursed her lips coquettishly. "There are things that need discussing."

Calico nodded. She too had important things to discuss. It was time to talk to Joy.

21

They sat outside in the courtyard in the tepid sunshine. It was odd, with all that Calico had been through these last days – the episode with the lift, the confrontations, the chase the night before – that she had never felt as uncomfortable as sitting here now beside her friend.

"What is it you wanted to say?" Joy asked eagerly.

Calico told her what had happened the evening before. Joy was horrified.

"Nemesis stalked you!" she breathed. "That's terrible. You must have been terrified. I would have been."

"It was pretty scary," Calico admitted. She eyed her friend uneasily. It was time for the interrogation to begin. "You spoke to my aunt yesterday, on the phone, didn't you? About a meeting…"

Joy nodded. "Dale wanted to meet up with Elizabeth McIntyre. He left me a message to call her."

Calico gently shook her head. "He didn't, Joy," she said, quietly. She wasn't enjoying this at all.

Joy looked puzzled. "He did," she said. "That's why I phoned."

"Dale couldn't have left that message," Calico insisted. She told Joy about the chairman's call. Joy appeared to be genuinely bewildered.

"I don't understand," she said with a shrug. "When I came back from lunch yesterday there was a message on my desk from Dale Jefferson to contact Elizabeth McIntyre at your aunt's flat and get her to come in for an important meeting."

"You didn't take the message, then?" Calico said.

"No," Joy confirmed. "I guess Fred or Dan must have done."

"Oh," Calico said, uncertainly.

"Is there something else?" Joy asked, picking up on her friend's evident unease.

Calico nodded. "I made some other discoveries last night," she said. She recalled for Joy her search in Romy's wardrobe and the unopened letter she'd found.

"Rose Marie Church had a child," Calico revealed. "It was adopted at birth. Marvin Adams was the father."

Joy's eyes opened wide in astonishment. "Wow," she muttered. She ran her hand through her bobbed blonde hair. "That's amazing. And you think this child might be Nemesis, right?"

"Yes," said Calico. "I think it's possible." She paused for an instant before continuing, "We don't know if the child was a girl or a boy. All we know is that he or she would be about twenty-two."

"My age," Joy said at once.

"Exactly," said Calico pointedly. She gave Joy a searching gaze. But Joy's soft blue eyes looked back uncomprehendingly.

"What?" she queried – and then, suddenly, the light dawned. "You don't think I'm Rose Marie Church's child? Why on earth would you think that?"

Calico's stare was unwavering. So this was it: the moment that she had been dreading since last night; the moment of accusation when a mystery might be solved, but a friendship destroyed. The moment of truth.

"Romy told me last night that Church was a pen name," she said gravely. "Rose Marie's real name was Sparrow."

Joy's face imploded with shock. "I-I-" she blustered. "You—" She stopped and took a deep breath, exhaling dramatically. She swallowed hard. "You're wrong, Calico," she said unsteadily. "You're wrong. I'm not Rose Marie Church's child." For several seconds she was overcome with distress and unable to speak. Then, gradually, she recovered some of her poise and, facing her accuser, she said, "My real name's not even Sparrow. It's Starling." It was

Calico's turn to look stupefied now. "You can look in the personnel files if you don't believe me," Joy continued. "I changed my name to Sparrow because there was already a Joy Starling on Equity's books. It's one of those sacrifices we actors have to make..."

"Your real name's Joy Starling?" Calico queried, bemused. It was all so strange. Was nothing as it seemed?

"Yes," Joy nodded. "My name's Joy Starling." Her face implored belief. "I'm on your side, Calico," she said, with a quick smile that revealed her dazzling white teeth. "I really am."

Calico's own smile was full of relief: her friend was not a murderer! She had nothing to do with Nemesis. Thank goodness! "Yes," she said happily. "I know, and I'm really sorry for doubting it, Joy. I can't say how sorry I am."

"It's OK, Calico," Joy said warmly. She leant across and put her arms round Calico. The two girls hugged each other.

How could she ever have suspected Joy? Calico wondered, as the friends walked back inside, arm-in-arm. Her refusal to accept the possibility of coincidence had led her to make a false assumption. She should have followed her instinct, she told herself toughly, which had informed her all along that Joy couldn't be Nemesis: she was a genuinely nice, open person, one of the most instantly likeable people that Calico had ever met. She just hoped their friendship wouldn't now be ruined.

Back in reception, Fred was on the switchboard.

"Where's Dan?" Calico asked. She wanted him to know right away that Joy was in the clear before there could be any more misunderstandings.

"I sent him off upstairs to collect the post," Fred intoned mournfully. He gave Joy an accusing look. "You should talk to me first, you know, before asking him to do something for you," he grumbled. "We're very busy."

Joy gave Fred her most brilliant smile. "Sorry, Fred. It won't happen again, I promise," she cooed, back to her chirpy self, it seemed.

"It was me who asked anyway," Calico confessed.

"Hmm," Fred grunted, but with more bark than bite. He got up off Joy's chair and gestured for her to sit down.

"Thanks, Fred," she said airily. "You're a gentleman."

As Joy took her seat, a light flickered briefly on the console before her. Standing behind her, Fred saw it and groaned. This time it was Calico who was the object of his disapproval.

"I warned you, didn't I?" he complained. "Your alarm's just gone off. Luckily, someone's switched it off, so the police may not pay it any attention. I'd better get on to them…"

"No! Wait!" Calico sprang out of her momentary stupor. In her relief at Joy's innocence, she'd allowed Nemesis to slip from her thoughts. "Don't ring yet, Fred," she implored. An icicle was forming along her spine, as she grabbed the nearest phone set and dialled the chairman's office. There were three interminable rings before anyone answered.

"Yeah?" a louche voice intoned.

"Mitch!" Calico squealed. "What's going on? Is the meeting still going on? Is Ms McIntyre there?"

Her panic was met with cool amusement. "Uh, well, like which question should I answer first?" he asked tauntingly.

"Just tell me, Mitch. It's important!" She was almost screaming now.

"Hey, chill it. The meeting's over," Mitch offered at last. "Dale's departed the building in a fury. Austen and the dragon have gone off together someplace to talk. I'm left to, like, pick up the pieces. Life's a bitch." Calico could picture the horsy smile on his face as she heard him bray with laughter. But it was the image of another face that was troubling her. As she slammed down the phone and swivelled to face Fred and Joy, she was recalling the look of intense hatred on Austen Porter's face as he emerged from Elizabeth McIntyre's office. "She's gone too far," he'd said. Another dark memory followed: *She has to go. And if she won't go voluntarily, then she has to be got rid of.*

"Get the police, Fred!" she commanded. "Joy, find Dan. Tell him I'm up in the reference library. Nemesis has struck!"

"But Calico—" Joy moved to try and delay her friend.

"Just do it, Joy!" Calico cried, the words flung out into reception, as she whirled about and ran.

22

She took the stairs two at a time, hands hauling on the banister rail, propelling herself up. Even so, it seemed to take an age to reach the top. Then she was through the fire door and into the lobby outside the reference library. She leapt at the door. But it was locked.

"Open the door!" she cried. "I know you're in there! Ms McIntyre, can you hear me?" Her pleas were met with an awful silence. "Ms McIntyre, Austen, talk to me, open the door!" she wailed, pummelling on the wood of the door. There was no response, but she heard something moving in the library. It sounded like something being dragged; immediately, she had a picture of Ms McIntyre's limp body being pulled across the floor. Nemesis had drugged her, as he'd said he would. Now he was preparing to kill her. Maybe he had already... No, no! She wouldn't believe that. Surely he hadn't had time. But unless she did something quickly, Ms McIntyre would soon be dead. No way would the police arrive in time. Where was Dan? She needed him, but she couldn't wait any longer. She'd have to act on her own.

"Hang on, Ms McIntyre!" she shouted. "I'll get you out of there. The police are on their way." The words weren't really for Ms McIntyre. They were a desperate attempt to try and stall Nemesis.

She ran out to the staircase and down to the next floor. Opening the window there, she pulled herself up on to the sill and stepped out on to the fire escape. The ladder was narrow and the drop considerable. She told herself not to look down.

A hard breeze tore at her hair as she climbed. When she looked up hair whipped into her eyes, so she focused instead on the brickwork before her. A bird flew by, cawing shrilly, and she had to stop for a moment to compose herself. Then steadily, rung by rung, she progressed, until, at last, the window to the reference library was there just above her. Drawing level with it, she peered in anxiously. There was a body slumped on the floor, facing away from her, almost entirely concealed by junk. There was no sign of anyone else.

She was in luck. The window was still open from earlier. She pulled it fully open and with a major effort dragged herself through. Her legs and arms were aching and her face was sore from the cold. She felt a little dizzy, too, from the climb. But the job was only half done, if that. Collecting her senses, she moved forward tentatively, glancing about, expecting any moment to have to repel an attack. But none came. She made her way unchallenged across the cluttered floor, until she came at last to the body. She looked down, took in the strawberry blond hair reddened with blood – and gasped.

"Dan!" she breathed in astonishment. She crouched down and turned him over. His freckly face was pale and his breathing laboured, but he was alive, thank goodness!

Hearing a footstep behind her, she wheeled quickly, losing her balance, so that for an instant her gaze was on the floor.

"Austen," she threw the word out as a feeler. But looking up, she was surprised to see not Austen Porter but Elizabeth McIntyre. She appeared as immaculate and elegant as ever except for one thing: in one hand was an ugly piece of metal tubing, streaked with blood; her other hand was held behind her back.

"Ms McIntyre!" Calico exclaimed. "You're OK! What's going on? Where's Austen?"

Elizabeth McIntyre's brow puckered. "Austen?" she queried sharply. "I've no idea where Austen is. In his office, I should imagine, fuming."

"But –" Calico was completely confused. "But Mitch said you left the meeting together," she said.

"We did. Then I came up here with Dan," Elizabeth McIntyre said with some impatience.

And now, suddenly, Calico began to see. She wished she didn't, but she did. The truth felt like a spike in her heart.

"Dan's Nemesis," she said quietly, head bowed. "He's Rose Marie Church's son."

Elizabeth McIntyre nodded. "Yes," she said. "Dan's the avenging letter writer. He blames me for what happened to his mother. So he decided to hound me. I suppose he thought he would destroy me, the way he believes I destroyed her."

Her face adopted the formidable expression that Calico had come to know so well. "He just didn't realize how tough I am. None of them did." As if in confirmation, Elizabeth McIntyre glanced at the tubing in her hand. Then, she let it drop to the floor.

Calico barely heard her boss's defiant remark, for her mind was in turmoil. Phrases spun up at her: "*The eternal eye sees through all*", "*Murder's quitrent*", "*The fly flop of vengeance*". "'*I'll be revenged for all*'," she muttered aloud. Then, bitterly, "I should have known." Dan had been open about his love of Jacobean drama. What a joke, Calico informing him of those odd quotes' source, when of course he knew better than anyone where they came from. As she looked down at Dan, her mind started piecing things together. Dan had been one of the last in the building the morning of the fire, Dan was the only one who had seen the "liftman", Dan knew all of Elizabeth

167

McIntyre's movements because she, Calico, had told him everything, included him in all her investigations. How he must have laughed inside!

"So it was Dan all along," she said heavily. "He sent the letter bomb. He started the fire, sabotaged the lift, murdered Judy Price – just to get at you, to scare you."

"Yes," Elizabeth McIntyre agreed. Then she half-laughed, but without amusement. "Well, not quite," she added. "He didn't murder Judy Price."

Calico's eyes widened. "He didn't?" she queried. "I don't understand."

Elizabeth McIntyre gave her assistant a steely look. "Dan had nothing to do with Jude's death," she said coolly.

"Then who killed her?" Calico asked, baffled.

"She asked to see me," Elizabeth McIntyre continued, as if Calico hadn't spoken, "the evening after that unhappy meeting with Marvin Adams and Nina Mallinson. She said she needed to see me urgently in private – no one else must know. She chose the place. And when I got there she talked about the take-over and that she had decided to back it. She was convinced it was the best thing for the company. The deal was too good to refuse, she said. She was going to vote for it and she wanted me to do the same." Elizabeth McIntyre paused and pursed her full lips determinedly. "She'd given in to them, you see," she went on, "Dale and Austen. I couldn't allow that."

"So what happened?" Calico prompted. She was starting to feel distinctly uneasy.

"We were on a bridge over the river and I gave her a push," said Elizabeth McIntyre matter-of-factly. "The water did the rest. She couldn't swim."

"You pushed her in and watched her drown?" Calico uttered, horrified. "She was your friend."

"She was siding against me," Elizabeth McIntyre said with an indifference that made the hair prickle on Calico's neck. "It was a happy coincidence, though," the editor added, "when that second manuscript arrived, mentioning the suspicious death of a company director. I'd seen the first manuscript, of course, on your desk." She looked down at Dan contemptuously. "The funny thing is, he probably thought the same," she said. "No doubt he thought it a real stroke of luck, Judy dying the way she did. It gave real weight to his threats without him actually having to carry them out. Only, of course, it didn't threaten me at all, because I was the one who'd killed her." Her expression became tighter, her eyes more focused. "I told you, didn't I, that I would stop at nothing to safeguard the future of Prairie Books? And my efforts have been successful. The take-over's been scrapped, the offer's been withdrawn."

Calico's head was reeling from these latest and most devastating revelations. "I never dreamt you'd go this far," she said incredulously. What was happening couldn't be real, could it? Surely, she was having some kind of nightmare. Elizabeth McIntyre gave Calico a penetrating stare. "This company is my life, Calico," she reasoned. "I'll go to any lengths to protect it." She nodded at Dan. "That's why he has to die."

"No!" Calico cried aghast. The nightmare was getting wildly out of control. "You don't need to kill Dan."

"Oh, yes, I do," the editor insisted. "I have to cover my tracks. It has to look like he tried to kill me and in self-defence, I killed him. I'll be a hero then, you see. They won't be able to touch me – Dale and Austen and all their cronies. They all wanted me out, dead. But, as you see, I'm very much alive – and kicking."

"I don't understand," Calico said, bewildered. "Are you suggesting the chairman and Austen Porter were in league with Dan? That they helped him?"

"Let's just say they did nothing to stop him," Elizabeth McIntyre retorted acidly. "His desire to kill me suited their purpose." Her youthful face softened suddenly into a surprisingly affectionate smile. "We put a spoke in their wheel, didn't we, Calico?" she said. "We'll make a very good team, you and I. I think you'll make an excellent editor." Of everything Calico had heard so far, this suggestion was the most incredible. She gazed at her boss in disbelief.

"You don't really believe I'd carry on working with you after all this?" she exclaimed. "You can't."

Elizabeth McIntyre's smile was undiminished.

"Oh, but I do," she said gently. "Prairie Books comes first, Calico, you know that. People can be replaced, a great publishing tradition cannot."

"No," said Calico decisively. "No. People's lives are more important than the life of a company. No business deal is worth killing for. Surely, you must see that."

"No, Calico, you're wrong," Elizabeth McIntyre answered, her smile gone now. "I took no pleasure in killing Judy Price but it had to be done and I'd do it again if necessary. And, sadly, I see it is necessary." As she spoke these last chilling words, Elizabeth McIntyre brought her hand out from behind her back, revealing a thick-bladed carving knife. "I'm sorry, Calico, I really am," she said regretfully. "But if you're not with me, then you're against me, as they say. And that means you have to die. You've discovered too much."

She stepped forward smartly, but Calico was already on her feet and backing away. She ducked behind a bookshelf and waited, heart pounding, for the next move. She didn't have to wait long. The knife blade plunged through a row of books, narrowly missing her shoulder. She cried out and ran alongside the bookshelves to the end, glancing back to see Elizabeth McIntyre appear in a gap at the centre, knife held out menacingly before her and advancing... Calico hurried on, turned the corner and, to her horror, found herself hemmed in by shelves on three sides. The only way out was the way she'd come in. She looked around for a weapon to defend herself with, but, apart from an old, worn armchair, there was nothing.

The knife appeared and, behind it, Elizabeth McIntyre, her face grim and determined.

"I have to kill you, Calico," she said. As she spoke there was a knocking at the reference library door. Voices called out. A surge of desperation lifted Calico. "The door's locked! Use the fire escape!" she shrieked. The commotion distracted Elizabeth McIntyre. She stood still a moment or two, as if debating which problem to deal with first. Then her eyes became focused again and she moved towards Calico.

In the brief delay, though, Calico's mind had fixed on a tool of defence. They were all around her, in fact: books, heavy ones at that. Swiftly she grabbed an armful from the shelf beside her and hurled them at her attacker. Taken by surprise, Elizabeth McIntyre was knocked to one side. She staggered and fell against the worn armchair. Without hesitating, Calico ran past her and back the way she had come. Rounding the long bookshelf, she collided with a stack of typewriters and banged her shin.

"Ah!" she yelped, hobbling away across the room.

She'd stepped over the prone figure of Dan and was making for the window, when she was halted by a groan behind her. Turning, she saw Dan rising groggily, pulling himself up on his elbows. Beyond him and approaching with alarming speed, was

Elizabeth McIntyre, her eyes steely as the blade in her hand, raised, poised to strike...

"Dan! Look out! Behind you!" Calico yelled.

Slowly, much too slowly, Dan manoeuvred his head around. The blow was already on its way. He lifted a hand weakly, but had no hope of protecting himself. He cried out as the blade penetrated his flesh, then, with a hoarse gurgle, he dropped to the floor once more. Calico gave a horrified yell.

"Don't make if difficult, Calico," Elizabeth McIntyre said quietly, stepping forward. Her expression was soothing, sisterly. In the soft light of the falling sun the highlights in her hair glowed, her dangling earrings glinted. She was stunning, dazzling. "I have to kill you, Calico," she said again, softly, "for the good of Prairie Books. You know I'm right."

Still in shock, Calico was almost lulled into submission by the dual effect of her boss's solicitous tones and her magnificent appearance; she was so powerful, so formidable that resisting did indeed seem futile...

It was the sound of voices outside that saved her. Hearing them, Calico snapped out of the spell that her attacker had momentarily cast on her. As Elizabeth McIntyre advanced, she retreated, until she reached the window and could step back no further. She moved along the wall until she came to another bookshelf. Then, eyes never leaving Elizabeth McIntyre, she felt for a book thick enough to act as a shield. Just in time, she found one, pulling it out as her attacker lunged. The knife plunged deep into the weighty tome, but couldn't penetrate through it. Calico shoved hard, letting go of the book, which crashed, with the knife still in it, to the ground.

But Elizabeth McIntyre wasn't beaten. She leapt forward and seized Calico round the neck with an agility and strength that totally surprised the younger woman. They tumbled backwards hard against the shelves, which wobbled as books fell from them, spilling over the floor. Calico's head was being pressed back forcefully into the gap between two shelves, the rough wooden edge of the lower one chaffing her neck. She could barely breathe. She lifted her hands to try and prize away the fingers that were squeezing her throat, but the grip was an iron collar she could not remove. She kicked out with her legs and found bone, but she was too close to cause any real injury. Her eyes were bulging now, her brain tight, throbbing. Airless, she felt herself fading, floating away...

And then, suddenly, *wham*! Something crashed against her attacker and the hands at her neck released. Her head came forward and free of the shelves just a split-second before the whole unit collapsed backwards. Gasping, she turned round. Her eyes took a moment or two to focus properly, but gradually they made sense of the wreckage. She saw the fallen bookshelf unit and two prone figures. One was Elizabeth McIntyre, whose head was concealed entirely by books and shelving; the other, now gingerly raising himself to his knees, was Mitch. He turned his head to look at Calico and, catching her eye, let his mouth widen in a horsy, slightly apologetic grin.

"Just in the nick of time," he said, pushing a flop of lank hair from his forehead.

Calico still couldn't speak, but wheezing, she inclined her head towards the motionless figure of Elizabeth McIntyre. Getting to his feet, Mitch walked over and lifted the books from the editor's head and body. He bent closer, touching, listening. Then he looked back at Calico.

"I think she's had it," he said with a shrug. "Her neck's trapped under a shelf, you know. I reckon it's, like, snapped."

He underlined his words with a gesture of his big hands. "I can't hear any breathing." His gaze continued on past Calico and his brow furrowed. "Is that Dan?" he asked. "Is he OK? What's been happening?" Calico regarded him with empty eyes.

"Which question should I answer first?" she said numbly.

23

"I never thought I'd be glad to see Mitch Lennon," Calico said. She was sitting in Romy's favourite Italian restaurant with her aunt and Joy. The busy restaurant was bustling with people and noise: the low chattering of voices, the light tapping of cutlery on plates and dishes. Waiters drifted between tables. Outside, in the street, a soft rain was falling.

"Thank goodness, it's all over," Romy said. She took her niece's hand in her own. "I'm very proud of you, Calico."

Joy nodded. "You're a real star," she agreed.

Calico smiled modestly, but said nothing.

It was over a month now since that nightmare encounter in the reference library with Elizabeth McIntyre. As Mitch had suggested, the editor had been killed by the collapsed bookcase, her neck caught and broken between shelf and floor. Dan Ryan had been more fortunate. The knife wound he had suffered narrowly missed his heart. He had lost a lot of blood, but after major surgery and a week in intensive care, he'd recovered. Despite Calico's detailed report to the police of her final conversation with Elizabeth McIntyre, Dan had not been charged. There was no evidence against him and the police preferred to think it had all been the editor's doing, dismissing her last words as the rantings of a crazy woman. But she wasn't crazy, Calico knew, not in the way they meant anyway. She'd known exactly what she'd been doing and why. She'd manipulated and out-thought them all. Calico believed her story: Dan was Nemesis all right and he'd intended to kill Ms McIntyre in revenge for her treatment of Rose Marie Church, his mother. At some point in those missing ten years, Rose Marie Church had found and re-adopted her son and filled him with hatred for Elizabeth McIntyre. As for the editor's suggestion of a conspiracy, well, the jury was out on that. The thing is, even if Dale Jefferson, Austen Porter and April Street hadn't actually committed any crime – and most probably they hadn't – they were still guilty in Calico's eyes. Guilty of deceit, selfishness, greed, malice…

But nobody came out of the whole Nemesis business with much credit. Even she, Calico, had reasons to be unhappy with herself – most of all for distrusting Joy, but also for being taken in so completely by Elizabeth McIntyre and, especially, by Dan. Dan. Alluring, deceptive, deadly Dan with those elusive sea-coloured eyes. He'd got off scot-free and, after a well-publicized altercation with his celebrated father, he'd returned to Ireland. Calico had heard nothing from him and nor did she wish to. He was a closed book as far as she was concerned, though it did bother her that someone so obviously mentally unsound should have been allowed to go free.

But Dan Ryan was the past. He was out of her life now and tomorrow she'd be on her way to South America. Dale Jefferson had offered her a permanent job at Prairie Books. He'd been very impressed with her, he'd said, but the feeling wasn't mutual. Prairie Books had not been a happy place for Calico. The only friend she had there was Joy and she was leaving; she'd got an acting job at last with a touring theatre company. No, Calico's future lay elsewhere. She might well return to publishing one day, but right now she wanted to get away. She was going travelling.

"I'll miss you, you know," Romy said. "I've got used to having you around."

"Don't worry," said Calico, grinning. "I'll be back."

The rain had stopped and a pale glow lit the window. In the gentle golden light, the resemblance between niece and aunt was more marked than ever. They could almost have been taken for sisters.

"Maybe you'll write a book about your experiences

one day," Joy suggested teasingly, then with a sly glance at Romy she added, "a novel perhaps." Calico smiled again. This time, though, it was a warm, un-inhibited smile, full of affection, for it struck Calico suddenly just how much she liked and respected these two people. Amongst all the untrustworthy people she'd come across these past weeks, here were two on whom she could count absolutely, who'd remained loyal, supportive, true. *Thank goodness*, she thought, *for Romy and Joy*. She shook her head, her thick dark hair shimmering in the light.

"No thanks," she said, laughing. "I'll just get on with living." Her emerald eyes narrowed thought-fully. "Fiction," she said with feeling, "has a nasty habit of coming true."

Look out for the spine-jangling new crime series from Malcolm Rose:

LAWLESS: Brett. Detective Inspector with a lot to prove. Biochemical background. Hot on analysis but prone to wild theories. *Dangerous.*

TILLEY: Clare. Detective Sergeant with her feet on the ground. Tough and intuitive. Completely sane. *She needs to be.*

THE CASE: 1. *The Secrets of the Dead*
Four bodies have been found in the Peak District. They're rotting fast and vital evidence needs to be taken from the corpses. You need a strong stomach to work in Forensics...

THE CASE: 2. *Deep Waters*
Colin Games has died after a bizarre illness. A post-mortem reveals no obvious cause of death, but the pathologist isn't happy. Enlarged liver, anaemia, heart irregularities – it all points to *poison...*

Join **Lawless & Tilley** as they pick over the clues. But be warned: it's no job for the fainthearted.

P●INT CRiME

If you like Point Horror, you'll love Point Crime!

Kiss of Death
School for Death
Peter Beere

Avenging Angel
Break Point
Deadly Inheritance
Final Cut
Shoot the Teacher
The Beat:
Missing Person
Black and Blue
Smokescreen
Asking For It
Dead White Male
Losers
David Belbin

Baa Baa Dead Sheep
Dead Rite
Jill Bennett

A Dramatic Death
Bored to Death
Margaret Bingley

Driven to Death
Patsy Kelly
Investigates:
A Family Affair
End of the Line
No Through Road
Accidental Death
Brotherly Love
Anne Cassidy

Overkill
Alane Ferguson

Deadly Music
Dead Ringer
Death Penalty
Dennis Hamley

Fade to Black
Stan Nicholls

Concrete Evidence
The Alibi
The Smoking Gun
Lawless and Tilley:
The Secrets of the Dead
Deep Waters
Malcolm Rose

Dance with Death
Jean Ure

13 Murder Mysteries
Various